THE BRITTLER SISTERS
BOOK FIVE

USA TODAY BESTSELLING AUTHOR

JOSEPHINE BLAKE

Publisher's Note: This is a work of fiction. Names, characters, places, and incidents either are the product of the author's imagination or are used fictitiously. Any resemblance to actual persons, living or dead, business establishments, events, or locales is entirely coincidental.

979-8-3302-9988-1

Published by Josephine Blake. *www.awordfromjosephineblake.com*

Cover Design by Covers and Cupcakes LLC. *www.coversandcupcakes.com*

Thank you for purchasing "Noelle" by Josephine Blake. Enjoy!

Chapter One

Manhattan, 1888

Noelle heaved a sigh as she clambered from the Brittlers' family carriage and stared down at its rear left wheel, which had sunk to its bearings in thick, dark mud.

The day hadn't gotten off to a very good start. Firstly, she had been forced to sit through a deadly dull lecture provided at the courtesy of her father's sister, who was visiting from England.

"Well, dear," the woman had begun, squinting across the breakfast table to the place where Noelle sat, her fork halfway to her lips. "What *are* we going to do with you?"

Noelle raised her eyebrows at her aunt. Aunt Meldrid was a straight up-and-down, beanpole sort of woman with an incredibly long nose. Something, Noelle supposed, must come in handy, as she spent so much of her time poking it into other people's business.

Noelle popped her fork into her mouth and took her time chewing, doing her best to ignore the steady tut-tutting that was issuing from across the table.

"It's just you now, dear," said Aunt Meldrid, still tutting and eyeing Noelle in the way one might examine a sprout in the garden tray that was refusing to grow. "Isn't it about time you settled down? I wish you would let me set something up with Arnold's great-nephew. He's close by and," she added, her bony cheeks pinching together as she grinned, "I'm told he's quite proficient at the clarinet."

Noelle had groaned at that point and glanced toward her father, who sat at the head of the table, his great fluffy mustache bristling behind his newspaper as he attempted to contain his amusement.

"Auntie, I hardly think that 'proficient at the clarinet' ranks very high on the list of qualities one might desire in a prospective husband."

"Alright," said Aunt Meldrid testily, sitting back in her seat and looking quite disappointed. "Why don't you inform us what sort of qualities do merit recognition on this fabricated list of yours?"

Noelle choked on her eggs.

"Yes," agreed her father cheerfully, slapping his paper down onto the table and turning toward Noelle with an entirely unhelpful amount of interest. "Do let's hear what my delightful daughter requires in a suitor."

Color flooded Noelle's cheeks and she glared at her father, who still looked as though he were refraining from laughter with immense difficulty. "Is this relevant?" she asked him through gritted teeth.

"Oh, I should think it's highly relevant," said Aunt Meldrid. "How else would we ever manage to delve into the depths of your rather opinionated young mind?"

Noelle set down her fork and folded her hands in her lap, praying for patience. "Well," she said, choosing her next words with care, aware that Aunt Meldrid would be analyzing each of them for a flaw that she could nit-pick to death. "I would say that kindness would have to be at the fore of the list."

"Is that so?" said Aunt Meldrid critically, as though she didn't think that kindness would be at all the sort of quality worth mentioning. "Will your future husband use his *kindness* to provide for you and your future children?"

"Perhaps," answered Noelle. She was goading her aunt now. She couldn't resist. The woman was insufferable. "I also believe that determination is a key concern."

"Well, now, there's something I can understand," grumbled her aunt. She reached forward and took a sip of tea from a dainty china cup, her pinky in the air. "A man must be determined to succeed in every endeavor."

"Including the winning of a woman's heart," Noelle added, nodding her head. Her aunt's brief expression of approval slid into one of complete exasperation. She opened her mouth to contradict her, but Noelle was already talking over her. "I mean," she said innocently, "take Father for example..." Thomas's smirk fell away at once and he gave Noelle a warning look. "He positively *refused* to hear the word *no* in his pursuit of our Mother. I do believe he followed her round all of London until she agreed to court him."

Her father's shoulders rose in an embarrassed shrug, and he suddenly became very interested in adding sugar cubes to his coffee.

"Round all of London?" queried Aunt Meldrid, and her beak-like nose turned to Thomas Brittler, her beady eyes fixing on him with all the sharpness of a hawk spotting a field mouse.

"Yes, well," Thomas blustered straightening his collar. "As you know, Samantha was involved in a number of charitable events through the season. I simply desired to accompany her."

"After she had already rejected you? Was she not otherwise engaged with her duties?"

Thomas's face grew red; he glared pointedly at Noelle, who grinned, fluttering her dark eyelashes. "What was it you said to her on your first meeting, Father? Didn't you tell her that..."

"That's quite enough talk on the subject, thank you very much," muttered Thomas, leaping to his feet. He cleared his throat and pulled his napkin from his shirt-front. "Yes, I'll see you both later," he said, his cheeks still red with embarrassment, and he stomped out of the room.

Noelle tittered and continued with her breakfast, unaware that her aunt's sharp featured face had turned back to examine her critically. "Another piece of toast?" she said, watching Noelle spread marmalade. "Don't you think you've had enough? Your figure certainly doesn't need any filling out."

Noelle scowled at her aunt, then she looked her straight in the eyes and took a defiant bite, making sure to crunch it as loudly as she could.

She frowned at the memory of these callous comments and smoothed her hand over her flat stomach. She wasn't heavy. Alright, she was a bit fuller around the hips and bosom than any of her three sisters, but they'd always screeched of how they envied her. She looked very like her eldest sister, Dianna, who was blonde and willowy with pleasant curves around her hips. Oh, darling Dianna. It felt as though everything had started with her. Noelle sighed again.

Her eldest sister had been gone for nearly two years, and one by one during that time, her other sisters—Sarah-Jane and Charlotte—had gotten married and disappeared. Well, that was what it felt like. They'd abandoned her to live their own lives with their perfect husbands, leaving her completely at the mercy of her mother, Samantha Brittler, and her Aunt Meldrid, who were practically the same person. Noelle loathed her aunt's visits, which had become more and more frequent after Charlotte's wedding in the Spring of 1886. Noelle had the impression that her mother had summoned her aunt so that they could work together to marry her off to whichever suitor they deemed most appropriate.

A sick feeling of ill-usage welled up within her and Noelle snorted. Marry her off indeed. None of her sisters had married just because they had been instructed to, and she was quite determined that she wouldn't be the one to break the chain.

Flummoxed and irritable, she focused her attention on the problem facing her.

"It's stuck good, Miss," said the footman, Kincaid, bending low to give the wheel another fruitless tug. "I'll need a half a dozen men to help me lift it back...."

Thunder rolled over the skies, making the world vibrate with its throaty roar, and Kincaid's next words were drowned out. Noelle held a hand over her eyes and peered up the dirt track in either direction as soft raindrops began to fall.

"I suppose we should begin the trek," she said dispiritedly. "Should we head towards home? Or towards the shops? Which do you think might be closest?" Wind whipped her skirts around her ankles as she spoke.

"Unfortunately, I think we're about half-way in betwixt them both, Miss," shouted Kincaid. "I don't like to leave you alone, but I can't ask you to ride all that way with me in this weather. Why don't you wait in the carriage? I'll bring someone back with me."

Noelle frowned and glanced into the dark interior of the coach. "It's a bit of a ways," she said doubtfully.

"I can manage it, Miss," said Kincaid, waving his arms and shooing her back under cover. "I'll be back as soon as I can."

"But—."

Kincaid had already slammed the door. Noelle watched him unhitch the horse and tear away into the downpour, her spirits sinking into the dark mud as quickly as the carriage wheels.

The weather showed no signs of easing. Noelle fidgeted in the damp interior of the carriage, leaning this way and that to gaze out of the fogged windows. If anything, the clouds overhead grew darker throughout the afternoon as the rain pounded relentlessly upon the roof. Noelle's stomach gave a low growl.

An hour later, the storm broke like a fever in the night and the clouds split open. Sunlight glimmered down onto the rain-drenched landscape and Noelle had to shield her eyes from the sudden glare. "Really?" she muttered, staring accusingly up into the restless sky, "make up your mind, won't you?"

Stiff from her long incarceration, Noelle threw open the door and stepped out into the muddy track. The surrounding landscape looked as though it had been sitting on the bottom of a lake. She glared up the road between the large factory fences on either side, searching in vain for a sign of Kincaid's approach. Nothing. At this rate, she'd never manage to get to the shops and back before her mother arrived home this evening, not unless she was willing to walk the rest of the way on her own.

This particular stretch of road was not one that was usually favored by Manhattan's wealthier inhabitants. Bordered by high, intimidating fences, it was well-traveled by the factory and mill workers, some of whom were certainly not the friendliest of sorts. Most of them were male immigrants from Germany or Ireland who had traveled to Manhattan in search of work. They were generally built of rough material, their language guttural and their manners crude. But as it was early on a Wednesday afternoon when Noelle had set out, she had never considered the route they had taken as potentially dangerous. Not until she heard the shrill whistle echoing over the damp air that signaled the start of the workers' lunch.

On the path ahead of her, gates swung open in the fence line and men dressed in grubby work clothes began pouring into the streets. Most of them, Noelle saw with relief, headed toward the high street, no doubt in search of a quick meal in the marketplace. A handful remained behind, perching themselves on curbs and overturned crates to dig their stained fingers into their lunch sacks with dubious expressions on their faces. A small group of two or three meandered towards the carriage.

"Looks like someone 'ad themselves a lousy morning," laughed one of them in a thick accent, pointing at the trapped wheel.

Noelle stepped hastily behind the carriage, hoping they would pass by without noticing her.

"Eh, Jeb, look at the size of those caps," said another voice. "Selling one of them would pay my rent for three months."

"Aye," said the Irishman, and Noelle saw three sets of heavy work boots halt on the other side of the carriage. "Aye, it would mine too. It'd be nice to have a wee bit of help now an' then wouldn't it?"

"You two keep a look out," growled a third voice, and to Noelle's horror, the third man leant down and began loosening the decorative hub caps on the rear left wheel.

"Excuse me!" she huffed, stomping around the side of the carriage. "I'd thank you not to make off with pieces of my carriage. What claim do you have on my hubcaps?"

The third man stood up so quickly that he rammed his head into the door handle. Rubbing it, he turned a furious glare onto Noelle, who realized her mistake as he straightened. All three of the men were large and brawny, and they leered at her with undisguised interest as she took a hasty step away from them.

"I reckon we have more claim on them caps than you do yerself, little miss," said the Irishman to the left. "When is the last time a pretty thing like you ever lifted a finger to do somethin' for herself?"

"You out here all alone, sweetheart?" said the broadest of the three men. He was massive, built like an ox, with bloodshot, baggy eyes, and at the moment, those eyes were wandering over her form with lecherous intent.

"No," said Noelle, glaring at the three men as they slunk towards her. "My man will be back any moment."

"Yer man? Surely you don't refer to yer husband as *yer man*?" said the second man, and he let out a wheezy chuckle.

"Look at her, Diggy," said the bear-like individual. "Pretty little thing thinks she owns the world. Any husband of hers would be bought and paid for just as well."

Noelle shook her head in disgust. "Regardless," she said, taking a few measured steps around the carriage and away from the mangy group, "as I said. He will be back any moment." She moved gingerly around the patch of mud that had taken her carriage captive and slid into the tilted seat. “Good day, gentlemen,” she added. She made to tug the carriage door shut, but a large meaty hand had taken hold of the handle on the other side, and its owner was holding it fast. Noelle froze as the hugest of the three men bore down on her, smiling in a self-satisfied way as he watched her struggle to latch the door.

“Now then,” he said evilly, “you wouldn't be wanting to be depriving us of your delightful company, now, would you?” And suddenly, his hand shot out. He took hold of Noelle’s wrist and shoved her forward with enough force to knock her to the floor.

“Careful, Jeb,” muttered the Irishman. “You don't know who you might be messing with.”

“Yeah, we best keep moving along,” agreed the other.

“Shut up, both of you,” growled Jeb. “Keep a look out.”

Noelle scrambled away from the bestial man as fast as she could. Reaching the opposite side of the carriage, she fumbled for the handle behind her back, her heart leaping into her throat as Jeb hoisted himself in after her.

He was grinning now, his teeth pulled away from his lips in a malicious snarl. “You’re awful pretty to be left here all on your own,” he murmured, stretching out a hand and grasping Noelle's upper arm. "What'd you say I keep you company until someone comes to fetch you?"

"Get your hands off me!" The sound was meant to be a shriek, but it came out as a breathless hiss, and it was cut off as Jeb clamped a rough hand down on Noelle's lips. She bit down. Hard. And tasted blood. Jeb cursed and snapped away his fingers. Noelle filled her lungs and let out a hair-raising shriek.

He was on top of her, his horrible scent filling her nose and then, suddenly, he was gone. Noelle was so startled that she laid still for a full ten seconds, her chest heaving, then she sat up. There was a scuffling sound outside the carriage and Noelle heard an *Oof!* It sounded as though someone had just punched her attacker in the stomach.

Noelle slid out of the carriage door, her heart still hammering in her chest, and was momentarily confused by the scene before her.

"What's all this? What's all this?" said a voice, and the man struggling with Jeb took an abrupt step back. Jeb straightened, looking furious.

"Henry," he said, turning to face a workman who was clearly a superior of some sort. "I was..." Jeb looked around for his mates, but the two men had already fled.

Noelle saw the scruffy pair glance back at Jeb as they turned a corner and vanished down a side street.

There were again three men standing in front of Noelle. One of them, Noelle noticed with a rush of nervous interest, was very handsome. His face was red with exertion, and Noelle blushed as she realized that it must have been he who had pulled Jeb off her. He had to be just over six feet tall. His face was long, and structured as though the Lord had taken it upon himself to paint a perfect jawline. His hair was dark, and, at the moment, his eyes were narrowed in fury. When he glanced in her direction, Noelle felt her breath catch.

"He was attacking her, sir," said her savior furiously. His dark eyes flashed back onto Jeb. Jeb looked mean. His hair was disheveled, and his face had turned a blotchy purple.

His superior appeared startled. "Is it true?" he asked, turning crinkled eyes onto Noelle. She nodded, tugging at her dress, trying to straighten it. She knew she must look an awful mess. And she noticed, as she lifted a hand to her hair-pins, that her fingers were shaking slightly. She felt numb, and rather cold.

"We'll see what the constable has to say about this," said the workman, and he seized Jeb by the collar.

"I ain't going to the constable, Henry Berkshire, I'll tell you that," growled Jeb. He yanked free of his boss's grip and turned to Noelle. "You ain't heard the last of me, Miss," he hissed, and he spat on the ground by her feet.

The man who had saved Noelle moved so swiftly, she nearly missed what happened. One second he was standing three feet away from her, and the next he had wrapped Jeb's neck around his elbow and pulled him into a headlock.

"I think you owe the young lady an apology," he said viciously as Jeb struggled.

"Could we have a bit of help over here?!" shouted the workman exasperatedly, waving his hands. Noelle looked around. Their little drama had drawn a small crowd of factory workers down the lane. Two men strode forward and seized Jeb's arms. He jerked away from them, and lunged at Noelle, who felt her fist fly up as though of its own accord. As her hand made contact with Jeb's nose, she felt—all at once—a sickening crunch, and a blinding pain in her fingers. Jeb dropped onto his knees, cradling his face in his hands.

"I think you broke it!" he squalled.

"I quite wish I'd done you more harm than that," Noelle muttered, shaking out her fingers to ease the sharp pain. "Will *someone* please remove this man from my presence?" She looked up to see every man present giving her a startled look, then, slowly, two men bent down and heaved the hulking Jeb to his feet.

"You ain't heard the last of me," he spat again, blood pouring from both of his nostrils.

"Yes," said Noelle, coolly, "You said that. Unfortunately, I must disagree. Goodbye, Mister Jeb."

She didn't pause to watch as Jeb was dragged away from her, still caterwauling to the high heavens.

Chapter Two

"Let me help you with that."

As the small crowd around them dispersed, Noelle's savior stepped forward. She had climbed back into the carriage one-handed and lifted her drawstring bag from beneath the seat.

"I'm sure I have a fan in here somewhere," she said. Much to her chagrin, she heard her voice tremble as she spoke. She could sense him standing over her, examining her, but she did not look up.

"You're in shock, Miss," said the man kindly. He crouched down in front of her to look up into her face.

Noelle smiled. "I'm alright," she said. "Thanks to you, it seems."

"I hope anyone else would have done the same," he said, and his eyes were twinkling up at her. "What's your name, miss?"

"Noelle," she responded, dazed. "And yours?"

"Kenneth Black at your service, Miss," he said. He held out his hand and Noelle shook it with her good one, feeling calluses and blisters on his palm. She looked down at it.

"What is it that you do, Mr. Black?"

He grinned at her. "Oh, a little of this, a little of that," he said. "My favorite pastime is rescuing damsels in distress."

Noelle laughed. "I don't doubt that," she murmured, feeling the heat of embarrassment creep up the back of her neck once more. A shaft of sunlight slid across their gently entwined fingers and caught her eye. She stared at it, watching the way their skin seemed to glimmer in the brightness, and enjoying the strangeness of his hand in hers.

There came the distant sound of a clock chiming noon, and Noelle was brought back to Earth with an unpleasant bump. A cloud shifted, and it was as though a curtain fell on a lit stage. She released Kenneth's hand and stood up so fast that a wave of dizziness washed over her.

"I have to go," she said, raising a hand to steady herself. "It's already noon. Mother will be back soon."

"Wait," said Kenneth. His eyebrows had shot up in alarm. "Where are you going?"

"I... er," she paused in mid-step. "Frankly," she said, I'm not even quite sure how to get there. My driver," she indicated the raised seat at the front of her carriage, "he went to hire a few men to come help pull the carriage from the mud. The horse couldn't budge it, but he thought perhaps... with a few extra hands," she waved vaguely in the direction of the rear wheel.

"Where is it you were heading?"

Noelle hesitated. "There's a small bakery on the other side of town. I believe it's called... La Petite... something..."

For some inexplicable reason, Kenneth smiled. "La Petite Paradis," he said, grinning.

"You know it?"

"By some odd coincidence," he said, offering her his arm. "I was heading that way myself."

Noelle stared at him. "You're having me on," she accused. She moved forward and laid her palm against his proffered forearm, noticing as she did so, that he was impressively well-built beneath the coarse wool of his coat.

"Not at all," Kenneth's grin made him look devilishly handsome in the afternoon sunlight. The corners of his lips twitched as he gazed down at her, as though he was trying desperately to conceal a delightful secret. "I take it you wouldn't object to my accompanying you?"

"Not at all," Noelle repeated, and she allowed him to lead her up the street, carefully avoiding the slick piles of mud and the curious glances from the workers as they headed back through the factory gates.

She tried not to glance up at Kenneth Black as they made their way onto the main, but she could hardly help it. Noelle was a romantic, as anyone who knew her would attest. Ever since she was a girl she had had the picture of her ideal mate fixed in her head. She had even drawn pictures.

"He'll be tall," she remembered saying to her older sisters as she lay on the drawing room floor, surrounded by a detritus of crumpled bits of parchment. "But not too tall. And his hair will be dark. We'll look so good together, he and I. He'll be dark to match my fair. We'll be like the sun and the moon." She sighed, her little stockinged feet kicking behind her in a dreamy sort of way.

Dianna sat down beside her, a brush in her hand. "I shouldn't think that the sun and the moon have a very happy marriage," she said, grinning as she pulled

Noelle up by her underarms and began running the brush though her long blonde hair.

Noelle folded her arms across her small chest. "What makes you say that?" she grouched.

"Think about it," said Dianna, just behind her ear. "The sun and the moon light up the sky, but when one enters the room, the other leaves. I don't think they're very happy with one another."

"Oh, no. You're wrong," said Noelle, spinning so fast that she knocked the brush from her sister's fingers. It skittered across the floor and came to a halt beside Charlotte's foot. "Don't you see?" she asked, her eyes wide. "They took it upon themselves to light up the sky. They work together to do it. And it's not that one leaves the room when the other enters. They take hours, just gazing at one another with the stars in between them. The sun lingers until the very last moment, just so she can keep her eyes on her husband. Their love is very great," she finished.

Charlotte snorted as she bent to retrieve the hairbrush and Sarah-Jane giggled, but Dianna smiled. "I stand corrected," she said.

Noelle was feeling very much like the sun as she strolled along beside Kenneth Black. Her face was glowing. She could feel the heat in her cheeks. He was perfect to the last hair. His features were sharp and square. Even his mannerisms pulled her toward him with some unknown force. It was irresistible, as though she had been waiting for him all along, but it had slipped her mind that they had arranged to meet long ago.

"So," he said, clearing his throat as he caught her eyeing him for the third time. "What is it you're looking for at La Petite Paradis?"

"I'm sorry?" Noelle had just noticed that Kenneth's eyes were a startling shade of green, and as such, completely forgotten that he was speaking to her.

He laughed. It was a deep sound, like thunder, and it went through Noelle like a fork of lighting. "At the bakery. Are you intending to place an order?"

"Oh, yes." Noelle attempted to gather herself. "It's my mother's birthday in a week," she said. "I want to order a cake."

"I see," said Kenneth. He still had that air of trickery about him, as though he knew something that she did not.

"Are cakes very amusing to you, Mr. Black?" she asked, a little confused.

"Well, everyone enjoys a good cake," he said. "I hear The Paradis has the best in town."

"A friend had a dinner party a few weeks ago, and mother was quite clear that it was the best cake she had ever had." She giggled. "I had to keep it from our darling cook. Something tells me that the idea would mightily offend her."

"I should think so," said Kenneth. He pointed ahead of them. "I hear this place has a few treats worth taking notice of though."

"I've been in there," Noelle said, glancing through the shop window as they passed. "It was delightful, but I'm afraid my mother is quite particular. She *will* ask me where I purchased the cake and will make no trouble to conceal her disappointment if it is not from La Petite Paradis."

Kenneth laughed again. "Well, it's a bit more of a walk," he said.

"I realize," she muttered, hiking up her heavy skirts as she stepped over a puddle. "But I'm afraid if I don't get there soon, the bakery will be closed, and this whole horrible day will be for naught."

"You chose a poor route," he said, and his face darkened. Noelle could tell he was recalling the predicament he had found her in.

She gave his arm a squeeze. "Thank you, again, for your assistance. I'm not sure what might have happened if you hadn't been there."

"Exactly," Kenneth said, unexpectedly sharp. "You ought to be more careful."

Noelle was affronted. "I didn't *intend* for the carriage to wind up stuck in that particular spot."

Kenneth looked down at her. "Some of the factory workers are vicious," he muttered, turning his head to stare ahead of them, unseeing. "You'd certainly be better off without mixing with them. Especially someone of your..." he hesitated, and Noelle saw his eyes dart over her form, "stature," he finished, although she was sure that hadn't been at all what he was thinking.

"My stature," she repeated, her pleasure in his company evaporating in an instant. "You think because I'm small that I cannot handle myself?"

Kenneth froze on the spot, and Noelle thought she saw him wince at her tone, but when he turned to look at her, his face was one of feigned surprise. "I would have thought that much was obvious, given the state I found you in."

"I could have taken care of that myself," Noelle growled, knowing perfectly well that she was lying through her teeth.

"Oh ho!" exclaimed Kenneth, his grin turning lopsided with skepticism. "Well, if it's true that you do not require my assistance, perhaps I should take my leave of you." With that, the infuriating man bobbed his head to her, and began to stride away.

"Wait!" Noelle cried out. "You can't leave me here." She clutched at her skirts and darted after him.

"So," Kenneth paused, eyeing her with his brow furrowed. "Are you admitting that you might need my help after all?"

"Of course I need your help," Noelle huffed. "You know the way to the bakery. Without you, I'd have to turn back around and wait for Kincaid by the carriage."

"If you could find the way, that is," said Kenneth with a smirk.

"I know the way," exclaimed Noelle, exasperated. "It's..." she spun on her heel, looking back at the way they had come. "It's... Oh, what does it matter? I'm not looking to go back. I have a cake to order."

"But how are you going to get there?" She could tell that the man was being infuriating on purpose and had to refrain from stomping her little foot with mounting frustration. "I thought you offered to accompany me," she said sourly.

"I offered to accompany a very polite young woman to La Petite Paradis. Unfortunately," he looked around mockingly. "She seems to have vanished."

Noelle frowned. "Perhaps if you hadn't climbed up into the saddle of a very high horse, I might not have reacted with such rancor."

"Is that what you call rancor?" laughed Kenneth. "I tremble at the thought of your scorn, my dear."

Noelle glared at him, her hands on her hips. Her little purse swung from her wrist, dangling in her skirts. "It seems we have reached an impasse," she said at last.

"It seems we have."

Noelle might have been less annoyed with him if he hadn't kept grinning at her as though she was in for some sort of treat. "Mr. Black," she said, taking a deep breath and squaring her shoulders. "Will you or will you not guide me to this little bakery?"

"On the whole, I think that I shall in the end," sighed Kenneth theatrically. He held out his arm once more, but Noelle was loath to accept it. She marched right past the man, doing her very best not to notice the enticing scent of cinnamon that seemed to fill her nostrils as she did so. Was he carrying sticks of the stuff around in his pockets?

"Miss?" Noelle halted and glanced back over her shoulder.

"We'll be going this way," he said, nodding his head at a little side street that she had not noticed up until that moment.

With another huff, she turned right around and stalked past him once more.

Kenneth let out an amused little chuckle that sounded as though someone was stirring melted chocolate around in a boiling pan.

"Are you always this infuriating?" she asked him over her shoulder.

"Are you always so easily infuriated?" he shot back.

Noelle did not respond.

They arrived at La Petite Paradis just as the sun had begun to sink into the sky. The shop was rather cute, Noelle had to admit. The bricks on either side of the door were covered in trellises that reached just below the roofline. Pink and white roses wove in and out of them in a tell-tale game of hide and seek.

The door was a magnificently prominent blue that stood out clearly against the dull shop fronts on either side, and through the window, Noelle could make out a variety of breads, sweet cakes and scrumptious sweets.

"I can't believe I've spent an entire day marching through muddy puddles in search of a cake," she grumbled.

"It does seem like an inordinate amount of effort to go through to please your mother," said Kenneth.

"Well, my mother is a difficult person to please," sighed Noelle. She could see a light on inside the shop, but when she reached for the handle of the door, she found it locked. "No," she muttered, jiggling the knob. "No, they can't be closed."

She took a step away from the door and pressed her nose against the display window, hoping she could signal whoever happened to be working behind the counter, but there was no one there.

Noelle groaned and took a step back, lacing her fingers behind her head. "I can't believe it," she moaned, looking up at the pleasant, hand-painted sign above the door. It let out a pathetic squawk as a slight breeze whispered through the quiet street.

"I have something that might help," said Kenneth cheerfully from just behind her.

"Unless you have an ability to contact the owner of this infernal establishment, I doubt that I will be very easy to impress."

"Well," responded Kenneth, scratching absentmindedly at the dark scruff around his jaw, "I don't think it would do us any good to contact the owner at this point."

"It's really not a bad idea," said Noelle, gaining enthusiasm for the idea the longer she thought about it. "Surely he can't have gone far. Perhaps to a nearby tavern or..."

"I can't contact him," said Kenneth approaching the place where Noelle stood, looking towards the bright bakery door with grim calculation, "but I can do you one better."

"Better?" sighed Noelle, her shoulders sagging with her disappointment.

"Much better," said Kenneth. It was then that Noelle caught sight of his face. The ridiculous man was grinning from ear to ear. He looked, if it were possible, even more amused than he had been all day. She scowled at him and opened her mouth. "You see..." he continued before she could speak, pausing for a moment to fish something out of his pocket. "I have the key."

It took a full five seconds for Noelle to process what he was saying to her. Kenneth Black continued to smile benignly as he inserted a small copper key into the lock and pushed open the bakery door. A small bell tinkled over his head.

"You..." she was at a complete loss. Something that was —in itself— an altogether rare experience. "You are the... the owner?" she asked, swallowing.

"Well, half owner," he clarified, looking rather pleased with himself.

"All this time," cried Noelle, wracking her brain to think if she had possibly insulted him in some way. "You let me walk with you all this way without bothering to inform me—."

"You never asked," said Kenneth with a little shrug. "Won't you come in?"

Seething with humiliation, Noelle stepped over the threshold as Kenneth held the door open for her. The air was warm. She could hear a small wood stove crackling behind a grate in the corner. A hundred rich, inviting scents filled her nostrils. It was intoxicating and overwhelming at the same time, rather like the man who closed the shop door behind her and stepped past her, pulling off his woolen coat and tucking it neatly beneath his arm as he went.

Noelle watched Kenneth with narrowed eyes as he slid around the three little tables crammed into the room, lighting the oil lamps and turning them up. As the rest of the bakery came into sharper focus, Noelle gasped. Rows upon rows of shelves lined the space behind the counter, each with a neat little label in that same hand-lettered style as the sign outside.

Fifty different kinds of breads, buns and treats were stacked in neat little rows behind the counter. A few reposed in glass cases; others were poked into linen bread bags.

"Tomorrow's bakes," said a voice from beside her. Noelle jumped. She hadn't heard Kenneth approach.

"You'll sell all of this tomorrow?"

"I'm still short a few loaves," said Kenneth proudly. "I've a few I need to check on in the oven now, and I'll make a few things throughout the day tomorrow when things slow down."

He walked over to the stone oven and used a hand mitt to open the metal grate. The smell of freshly baked bread flooded into the bakery, and Noelle heard her stomach give a low growl. She gave a small cough to conceal the noise, but Kenneth wasn't fooled.

"What have you eaten today?" he said suddenly, frowning as he used a large, flat shovel to scoop two bread pans onto the countertop.

Noelle felt her brow furrow as she tried to think. What had she eaten today? Her stomach growled again, and she folded her arms over it with embarrassment.

Kenneth glanced up from his loaves and gestured her over to him with an expression that dared her to try and disobey. She came, partially because Kenneth looked as though he might force her to his counter at the point of the butter knife in his hand, and partially because the smell of the bread was already causing her mouth to water.

"Come here," he said, tugging a barstool out from behind the counter and setting it down beside him. When Noelle raised her eyebrows at him, he added a "Please," with much rolling of his eyes. She sat, her eyes now fixed on the two delicious loaves of bread that Kenneth was slicing into with a certain finesse. "I'd normally allow them to cool for a while yet," he said as Noelle's stomach gave another low growl, "but I think in this case I'd better make an exception." He chuckled as he passed her a buttered piece.

Noelle accepted it with thanks and raised it immediately to her lips. He was watching her. "Do you always stare at your customers while they eat?"

"Are you a customer?" joked Kenneth, his expression one of innocent bewilderment. "I had no idea. Here I was thinking you were just a pretty girl with the stomach of a lion."

Noelle laughed, and then, unable to resist for another second, she sunk her teeth into the delicious, warm, softness before her. Kenneth never took his eyes off her face. She could feel him watching her as she closed her eyes in ecstasy. She took her time chewing, and only after she had swallowed, did she look up again.

"That," she said, dabbing at the corner of her mouth with the napkin he handed her, "is the best thing I have ever tasted in my life."

Kenneth laughed, but he looked positively delighted with her reaction. "It's only because you're starving yourself. That is nothing more than regular old wheat bread."

"It's amazing," Noelle insisted. She took another bite.

For a few moments there was silence except for the peaceful crackling of the fire and the gentle saw of the bread knife in Kenneth's hand. Noelle watched him with interest, the ravenous monster in her belly only briefly pacified. His hands were gentle, but firm, just like his manner. He had the long tapering fingers of an artist, and the skill to accompany them.

"You enjoy what you do," she whispered after a time. It was a statement, not a question. Kenneth's passion for his craft was evident.

The room was quiet. It felt as though they were the only two people in the world.

"Very much," replied Kenneth. He smiled as he dipped the end of the loaf into the butter dish and popped it into his mouth. "There's a bit of science to it, you see. A bit of art too. The things I make need to be beautiful, so that people want to buy them, but they need to taste good too, so that they want to come back."

"I'd say you're doing a bang-up job of that," said Noelle, staring at the remaining slices of bread and wondering if it would be polite to ask for a second one.

Her companion seemed to read her mind, because he handed her a buttered slice before she'd even managed to open her mouth.

"Thank you," she said gratefully, taking the slice and watching as he buttered another for himself.

"I'll be right back," he muttered with a mouth half-full of bread.

He returned a moment later with a round of cheese and a cured ham. "Sandwich?" he offered, indicating the cheese.

"I can't let you empty your cupboards for me," said Noelle, although her stomach had contracted with sudden excitement.

Kenneth laughed again. He seemed to do that quite a lot. Or perhaps he simply thought her ridiculous. She couldn't decide. "I don't think that's possible, young miss," he said. He drew up a second barstool and they began slicing ham and cheese in a companionable silence.

Every now and then, Noelle glanced at the window. The sky was turning indigo as it began to set behind the vast dwellings on the opposite side of the road. She wondered briefly if Kincaid would be able to find her. Surely, he would guess where she had gone when he returned to find the carriage empty. She felt a sudden lurch of anxiety for him. He should have been here by now.

"There," said Kenneth, passing Noelle a plate.

"If you continue to ply me with food, you may have to roll me out the door at the end of the night," she giggled.

"I'm a baker, miss," he said. "It's what I do."

Noelle gave an appreciative chuckle. "How did you come in to this line of work?" she asked.

"It sort of fell into my lap," said Kenneth, smiling at her obvious interest. He stood and filled a glass of water from a silver pitcher in the corner. "I don't think I ever intended to have my own shop, but-."

He was cut off as the shop door opened with a loud squeak, sending the bell above the door tinkling again. Noelle looked up at the newcomer, half-expecting it to be Kincaid, and quite prepared to order him to wait for her in the carriage until she was through. Despite the glumness of the events of the day, with a full belly and a handsome man to converse with, she was beginning to quite enjoy herself.

She was surprised therefore to discover herself face-to-face with a young woman, perhaps a bit older than she, with dark hair and a very pretty face. Her nose and jaw both tapered to sharp little points that were not unbecoming. The effect was sprite-like, and at the moment, she looked rather as though she were ready to lay a curse down upon anyone who crossed her.

"Kenneth Black, where have you-?" she stopped as she caught sight of Noelle. "Oh," she said, her cheeks flushing a darling shade of pink. "I'm sorry, I didn't realize we had a guest."

Noelle stood up abruptly. "I should be leaving," she said uncomfortably. It had never occurred to her that Kenneth was married. He certainly hadn't behaved as such. She felt a momentary rush of embarrassed fury. And he had carried on with her… flirting and smiling and leading her to believe…

"Please don't leave on my account," said the woman. She was carrying a box of what appeared to be vegetables on her hip, but she deposited this on the counter and stepped towards Noelle with a warm smile.

Noelle noticed her eyes flash curiously between Kenneth and herself, and she swallowed her unease quickly, so as to appear unperturbed. "Cynthia Black," the woman said, holding out her hand in greeting.

"Noelle Brittler," Noelle responded. She glanced over her shoulder at Kenneth, who, she was pleased to see, was looking slightly ashamed of himself.

"I'm sorry, Cynthia," he mumbled, avoiding her eyes. "I lost track of things today." He was rubbing the back of his neck.

"That's quite alright," said Cynthia, her eyes still darting between them. Noelle had the impression she was sizing her up, analyzing everything from the wretchedly muddy state of her dress to the dull flush in her cheeks. Noelle was feeling increasingly uncomfortable. What had she been thinking? She'd never bothered to ask… but he wasn't wearing a ring…

Her mind was skipping around as though it had landed on hot coals. There was an awkward silence. Noelle could have cut the tension with a knife. Then, suddenly, with more relief than she thought she had ever felt in her life, Noelle spotted something outside the bakery window.

"Ah," she said, exhaling, "I do believe my carriage has arrived." She nodded in the direction of the window, where she could make out Kincaid leaping from his perch, evidently in a terrible state of worry.

"Thank you very much for your hospitality, Mr. Black," she said hurriedly. She reached into her purse and withdrew a handful of coins. "For the meal," she muttered, not meeting the Baker's eyes. She set the coins on the counter and turned to his wife. "It was a pleasure to meet you, madam," she said.

"Miss Brittler-." Kenneth began to speak, but Noelle was already out the door. She pretended not to hear him calling out to her as the bell tinkled and the door slammed shut behind her.

She was in such a hurry to get away from the Blacks that she nearly walked straight into Kincaid.

"Thank heavens!" he exclaimed, grabbing her by the shoulders. He looked as though he was about ready to throw his arms around her, but thankfully, he resisted.

"I'm so very sorry, Miss. I nearly had heart failure when I realized-."

"It's fine, Kincaid. Completely understandable. But I would like to head for home straight away, if you don't mind."

"Of course, Miss." Kincaid pulled open the carriage door, glancing curiously back at the bakery as he did so. "Are you alright?" he asked in a whisper.

"I'm very tired, Kincaid. Won't you please hurry?" She was anxious to set off before Kenneth could come after her.

She climbed into the carriage just as the bakery door tinkled again. "Miss Brittler!"

"Drive on, Kincaid," Noelle whispered under her breath, hoping against hope that he would hear her. But whether the footman heard her or not, she felt the carriage give a sudden jolt, and then they were trundling away up the street, her heart rather sick and her stomach tied in knots.

Chapter Three

Kenneth watched her go with his chest heavy with disappointment. What on Earth had caused such an abrupt change in her demeanor? The moment that Cynthia had walked in... he wracked his brains as he reentered the shop, his shoulders slumped.

"I'm so sorry," said his sister, her thin fingers—so very like his— against her mouth. "I didn't mean to scare her away."

"It's nothing," said Kenneth waving his hand and trying to hide his dejection.

"Was she a customer?"

"In a manner," he said, smiling wryly. In a few short minutes, he recounted how he had come upon Miss Brittler. He left out the absolute fury that had driven him to her aide, and the immediate attraction he had felt towards her, despite knowing full-well that she was entirely out of his reach.

"Perhaps it's for the best," said Cynthia, laying a consoling hand on his arm. "A Brittler, Ken? She was bound to be horrible."

"Why? Because she has wealth?"

"Girls like that are used to getting whatever they want from whomever they want."

"I don't think she was like that at all. And apart from that, have you ever heard one bad thing about Thomas Brittler? Just because a family has money doesn't make them cruel."

"Perhaps you've had different experiences with the upper-class than I have," said his sister grimly.

Kenneth shook his head. "I liked her," he said with a small shrug. He was looking towards the fire, which was beginning to dim in the grate.

"You like everybody," laughed Cynthia, giving him a small nudge. "Cheer up," she said. "What's a girl like her going to have to do with a lowly Baker boy anyways? You don't want a snobbish one. Come help me lug in the rest of our order."

This brought Kenneth out of the fog with a jolt. "I'm really sorry. It completely slipped my mind," he said, following her outside. He was the one who was supposed to pick up their monthly orders from the mercantile. It was his job, not Cynthia's.

He could practically hear his sister rolling her eyes. "I left it in the note on the counter this morning," she grouched.

"I know. I saw it. It was the whole..." he waved his hand vaguely toward the place where Noelle's carriage had sat only moments before, and his face darkened. Why had she run away like that? Had she been embarrassed? Truth be told, he'd thought they were getting on rather well. "It had me hanging upside down by my ears."

Cynthia snorted as she turned down a tiny alley beside the shop. "You mean *she* did," she barked. "Honestly, Ken, one would think you'd never seen a pretty girl before."

Kenneth frowned, but made no comment. Reacting would only confirm the truth to Cynthia, and Lord knew she didn't need additional ammunition with which to tease him.

"Am I alone in thinking that she reacted strangely when you came into the shop?" he asked, not really expecting a response. "I mean," he said, dragging his feet along the stone path. "What was going on? We were getting along fine until you came butting in."

Cynthia scowled at him, but did not honor him with a retort. Instead she shrugged, and moved away from him.

Their small cart was parked just around the corner. Their horse, a brooding gray mare, turned dark, glassy eyes on them as they approached. It took them a little over ten minutes to unload.

Once they had stowed the cart and horse, they moved into the shop and began sorting through the various boxes. "Have you spoken to Margaret?" Cynthia asked him when they met at the ice box, both carrying perishables.

Kenneth groaned. "Why is it that, whenever the subject of myself and a woman turns up, you have to go and bring up Margaret?"

Cynthia grinned. "She's been asking about you."

He groaned again. Margaret Piper was the daughter of a seamstress who owned a little boutique on 7th Street. Under the combined influence from his sister, the girl's mother, and Margaret herself, Kenneth had organized a small picnic in Central Park, placing himself at the mercy of three women who were quite eager to marry him off.

"I did it once because you told me too," he said, his voice carrying a hint of an Irish burr. "I'll not be doing that again."

"Whoops, my dear brother, I do believe your Irishman is showing a touch," said Cynthia on a laugh.

"Rubbish," he grumbled, and he returned to his task. "What about you, then?"

"What about me?" retorted Cynthia, stretching up onto the tips of her toes to pull a small box from the top shelf. As she tottered, Kenneth caught the box and grinned. "What about you? Have any of the fine gentlemen caught your eye as of late?"

Cynthia scowled up at him. "It's not any of your business," she said, reaching for the tin in his hand, but Kenneth held it just out of reach.

"What about that nancy-boy at the market? He was friendly last week."

His sister hopped on the spot, attempting to wrest the box from his fingers. "His name," she huffed on mid-jump, "is Timothy," she finished as her tiny feet touched down again. "Give me that!"

Kenneth held the box higher still. "Oh Timothy, oh Timothy, your heart is so true!" he sang in a high-pitched, sing-song voice.

"Stop, you miserable cad!" cried Cynthia, laughing as she covered her ears, but he sung louder still. "Alright, alright, he's nice to look at. Are ye happy now?"

Kenneth lowered the box, grinning down at his tiny older sister. "My dear sister," he said, giving her a playful poke in the ribs. "I do believe you sound a wee bit Irish!"

Later that night, as he was lying in bed, listening to the sounds of the city, which never really did seem to sleep, his mind returned to Noelle. To say that he had liked her would have been a remarkable understatement. She had been friendly, witty, and improbably stubborn, and that was on top of the fact that she was the most beautiful woman he had ever seen. Her hair had seemed to glow in the brief patches of sunlight, and she had seemed to reverberate with boundless energy, even after her narrow escape.

He would have expected her to faint with shock, or even to cry after what had happened. But no. She had leapt up and... he recalled, with a rush of pure satisfaction, the sight of her walloping that horrid man right in the nose, and he nearly laughed out loud.

He believed she could have fought her own battles, with a fair and fighting chance. She was quick-witted enough. Nothing like he would have expected a Brittler girl to be. Nothing at all.

A low snore echoed from Cynthia's room next door, and he thought about what she had said. "What's a girl like her going to have to do with a lowly baker boy?"

She was right, of course. Kenneth sighed, shaking his head. Even if she'd had the most beautiful smile in the world. Even if her laugh had sounded like the sweet chime of his shop bell. They were of completely different classes.

Still, Kenneth thought, rolling over to stare out of the second story window of his room. She hadn't acted as though there were any difference between them at all. He sighed again, grumbling to himself.

And then another thought struck him. One that yanked him out of his melancholy, self-pitying state and made his mouth split open in a wide smile.

She hadn't remembered to order a cake.

Chapter Four

Grumbling to herself, Noelle pulled dress after dress out of her wardrobe. Simple dresses in fine linen, elegant soiree gowns in light, airy silks. She'd tried them all, and everything in between, but not one of the dresses in her closet was fitted for an occasion such as this. She wanted to appear in La Petite Paradis with a look that said: "Here I am. I'm angry. You are a wretched man. Now give me a cake."

A knock sounded on her bedroom door. "Miss? Would you like me to come in and do up your laces?"

"Not yet!" shrieked Noelle, close to tearing out her hair in frustration. She gathered herself and then repeated: "Not yet, Alice. I'm sorry. Give me another moment."

She listened to the sound of her lady's maid walking away down the hall and turned to face the disaster that was her room. Her entire closet was splayed out over the antique carpet. Her mother would be absolutely mortified.

"You made the mess," she said to herself, lifting a gown and sliding it back onto the hanger. "You're not going to ask Alice to come in here and clean it all up for you."

If only she had a magic wand. This was a thought that often occurred to Noelle. A magic wand or a fairy godmother. Something of the like. Something that would take the fluffy piles of silk and taffeta surrounding her and turn them into exactly what she needed. As she replaced each dress in her wardrobe one by one, she caught sight of something out of the corner of her eye. It was a packing case tucked away beneath her bed. The sight of it saddened her for a moment, because it made her think of Dianna. It made her think of her eldest sister packing away her life to go on an adventure. At the time, Noelle had saluted her sister for her nerve, but in times like these... when she desperately needed help and advice... Noelle shook her head and continued with her task, lifting a velvety evening gown from the floor. But then an idea struck her. An unusual but potentially wonderful idea.

Without a moment of hesitation, she darted out into the hallway and ran smack into Alice. Her handmaid stared at her, clothed as she was in nothing but her underthings. "Miss?" she asked, a note of trepidation in her voice, as though she feared that Noelle had gone mad.

"I'll just be another moment or two," said Noelle, and then she launched herself across the hall and into Dianna's empty bedroom.

When Dianna had packed all her things to travel West, she had left several dresses behind. Noelle distinctly remembered Charlotte attempting to pack them in her trunks, and Di had said "When on Earth would I wear it?"

With a shiver of excitement, Noelle pulled open her elder sister's wardrobe. Dust shifted in its nearly vacant depths, and she had to wave a hand in front of her face. There it was. That would do the trick.

Reaching forward, she grasped the soft fabric and allowed it to tumble from the hanger. It was rose-pink with shining floral laid into the satin, and it slid over her fingers like water, perfectly supple, despite its nearly five years of disuse. Would it fit?

Although they looked very much alike, Noelle was a bit shorter than Dianna, and her figure was rounded in places where Dianna's was slim. Pulling the dress from the wardrobe amidst a small dust cloud, she held it up to herself and gazed over the Persian carpet to the mirror that stood on the other side of the room. "Only one way to find out," she muttered to herself, and she lifted the gown up over her head.

She stood there for about the space of ten seconds, her eyes closed tight, and when she opened them, there she was. Her mouth fell open in shock. It was as though she had stepped into the future. Gone was the adolescent look that had haunted her features for much longer than any of her sisters. Gone was the youngest Brittler daughter, unmarried and overlooked. No. She was not that girl anymore. If anything, if anyone... she was Dianna. Strong. Level-headed, and yet so very, very brave.

"Noelle, what are you...?" her mother's voice hitched in mid-sentence as she pushed open Dianna's bedroom door. Her hand flew to her throat. "My stars," she said. Her eyes were wide. As Noelle watched, her mother tottered slightly where she stood and then, out of nowhere, tears began pouring down her cheeks.

"Mother?" asked Noelle, startled. She made to move forward, but she tripped on the over-long hem of the gown. "Mother, what—?"

"Forgive me, darling," said Samantha Brittler, her voice was uncharacteristically soft. She plodded over to the bed and sank onto the comforter, wiping hastily at her eyes and unwinding a small handkerchief from her pocket.

"I'm sorry. It's just... for a moment... I thought..." She shook her head, and blew her nose into the white cloth. Noelle lifted the dress and came to sit down beside her mother. The springs of the bed gave a little squeak.

"You thought I was Di?"

Her mother looked at her, and her smile was sad. Noelle had very rarely seen her mother like this. Perhaps a handful of times in the last ten years. Samantha Brittler was anything but emotional. But, then again, she'd changed a little bit as each of Noelle's sisters had grown up, married off, and moved away. She was still firm, still unfailingly rigid, but her eyes had lost some of the hardness she'd had for as long as Noelle could remember.

Noelle lowered her head, and strange though it felt, she rested her cheek on her mother's thin shoulder, feeling the coarse material of her dress scrape her skin. "I miss her too," she whispered.

Samantha's chest heaved in a sigh, and after a moment, she laid her hand over Noelle's. Her fingers were cold at that first touch, but it seemed to Noelle, that her hand warmed her mother's. She felt her fingers contract slightly, and she sat in silence with her mother, sharing an unfamiliar moment of kinship and quiet.

"Well," said Samantha at last, giving Noelle's fingers a strange little pat. She straightened and took her by the shoulders, looking her up and down. "Why don't you give that to Alice and see if she can take up the hem?"

Noelle nodded, and like that, the moment was broken. She could almost see her mother's walls stacking back up like bricks. She remained on her sister's bed as Samantha ran her hands over her own dress, removing any creases in the fabric, and then she cleared her throat and said: "Yes. Hmm. Well, I best get back to it."

Noelle felt a little flare of panic; she didn't want to have hurt her mother by trying on Dianna's clothes. "I'm sorry," she whispered to her back as Samantha made to exit the room.

Her mother stopped, her hand on the door frame, and then she looked back over her shoulder. "You look very lovely, my dear," she said, and with that parting note and a strange, crooked grin on her lips, she left Noelle alone, sitting on her eldest sister's bed, and listening to the echoes of the past.

As per Noelle's request, Kincaid had taken an alternate route through the city to reach La Petite Paradis. The day was at complete odds with Noelle's mood. Radiant sunlight fell over the dusty shopfronts as they passed, while inside the carriage, Noelle sat with her arms crossed over her stomach, biting her lip and second-guessing her decision.

It wouldn't have cost her anything to send someone to the bakery to place the order for her mother's birthday cake. Nothing except a chunk of dignity and pride, and possibly a few nights of decent sleep. She *could have* sent someone in her stead, but then she would never be able to look Kenneth Black directly in the eye and tell him without words that he was a rather despicable human being.

She still could hardly believe the way he had led her on. She had been *flirting*. Quite shamelessly in fact. And oh... dear...what would her mother say if she found out?

She will not find out, Noelle scolded herself. Although Noelle suspected that *if* her mother ever did discover that she had been associating with Kenneth Black, her fury would be less for the fact that Noelle was flirting with a married man, and more to the fact that he was a *Baker,* rather than someone of quality, as Samantha would put it. At this thought, Noelle rolled her eyes to the ceiling. Her stomach, already tied in knots at the thought of what she was about to do, erupted into a flurry of fairy-dust as she spotted their destination up ahead.

The Paradis stood out against the surrounding shopfronts. Not only was it the brightest display, what with the roses climbing around the red brick and the brilliant blue of the front door, but it also appeared to be the busiest shop on the street. People thronged around the little building. Some waiting in line, others having perched themselves at a small table or upon a nearby curb to devour their purchases.

Having expected the quieter atmosphere of her previous encounter with Kenneth Black, she was a little flummoxed. She had been intending to march into the shop, remaining aloof and unapproachable, and demand a magnificent cake from the man, all the while fixing him with a cold stare that told him *exactly* what she thought of his behavior.

Now though, she would have to wait in line. He was bound to see her coming, and have plenty of time to prepare a reaction to her presence. Noelle huffed as the carriage pulled to a halt. Might as well get this over with.

The sun beat down on the back of her neck as Kincaid slapped the reins and the carriage moved off around the corner, leaving Noelle alone on the street opposite the bakery. She was a tad over-dressed for a simple run into town, but at the same time, she enjoyed the way people were looking at her. She wondered if she should have some sort of story available to explain her outfit. Perhaps she was heading to the shops with some friends afterward, or meeting the president of the children's charity for luncheon. She giggled to herself.

The president of the children's charity was a rather deaf old woman who cherished a love of fine brandy. While she was very well meaning, she was also known to proclaim loudly about shapes of the clouds in the sky. Noelle liked her quite a lot.

Sobering herself, Noelle waited for a passing cart and then proceeded across the street to take her place in line against the creeper-covered brick. Heads turned as she moved, and Noelle pretended not to notice. It was empowering, to be seen. She wondered what all these people were thinking. None of the women in front of her were dressed in anything out of the ordinary. A few feet along, Noelle spotted a woman in a rich, purple riding habit. She had dark hair, and wore a black hat with a feather protruding from the top.

Noelle listened to the little bell above the shop door tinkling, and tried her best not to let her nerves sneak up on her. She was cool. She was collected. She was... Oh Lordy, there he was.

Kenneth Black had just stepped out of his shop, and either Noelle had forgotten just how handsome the man really was, or he had grown more so over the last few days. His chin was clean-shaven, but dark with afternoon stubble, and his scorching green eyes were lit with a bright enthusiasm.

He smiled and waved at his line of customers who were obviously regulars. They called out to him in cheerful, friendly voices, and Kenneth responded with equal ardor. *Every bit the salesman,* thought Noelle.

"Just running down the lane," he said to his spirited clientele. "Cynthia will take care of you all while I'm gone. I'll be quick, I promise!" And then, with a hearty wave, he jogged off down the street.

Noelle tried not to let her disappointment show. *He never even looked at me.*

Her heart had leapt into her throat at the sight of Kenneth, but now it had dropped right down past its usual spot and settled somewhere around her navel. She sighed, perspiring slightly in the heat, and looked around at the crowd.

She wasn't the only person who appeared to be disappointed at Kenneth's departure. The woman a few places ahead of her in line was looking rather downcast. Who was this then? Another of Kenneth Black's flirtations? Was she perhaps his mistress? Noelle eyed the woman up and down. If Kenneth's behavior with her had been any indication, he clearly enjoyed the company of a woman. But his wife... Cynthia. She hadn't appeared at all jealous when she walked in on he and Noelle's cozy little picnic. If anything, she had looked embarrassed, as though she was the one in the wrong. What an odd relationship. What a despicable man.

The line moved forward. Noelle was standing beneath the red and white striped awning that hung over the few scattered tables outside, and she could just see little Cynthia Black through the doorway, flittering around behind the counter as though she did indeed have wings. Where had Kenneth gone? How could he leave his wife to tend to all these customers alone? What a despicable man.

Noelle had to keep telling herself this. Because the way that her heart had leapt at the very sight of him had nearly made her forget the very thing that she had come here to achieve, apart from ordering a cake, of course. That was the main reason she was here... of course. It had little to do with putting Kenneth Black in his place. How dare he? She still couldn't believe it. The man ought to be locked up. With eyes like that... he was dangerous.

She was inside the shop now, and unfortunately, it was scarcely less hot in here than it was standing beneath the direct sunlight outside. She fanned herself idly while she looked around. La Petite Paradis was truly a magnificent shop. The shelves were all painted in bright primary colors, interspersed with white. While not very practical, the overall effect was quite charming. And Cynthia, darling, sweet Cynthia with the rotten husband, she was a delight. Her smile was welcoming and innocent and she looked incredibly happy. Yet how could she be? It was an impressive façade, it had to be. How could anyone be happy with a husband who dallied with other women on the side?

A wry thought struck Noelle then... Perhaps she truly didn't know? Noelle watched the little pixie of a woman for a moment, and concluded that that had to be the case. She was much too happy. Oh no. Oh dear. Someone would have to tell her.

Not me, Noelle chastised herself. *It certainly won't be me. I won't be the one to ruin her happiness.* The woman in the purple riding habit had approached the counter now.

"Margaret!" Cynthia exclaimed, with every appearance of delight on her face. "I didn't expect to see you today. And my you're looking lovely."

The woman, Margaret, did a little twirl. "You like it?" she asked with a small wink. "Mother just finished it this morning, so I thought I would come out on a little jaunt."

"Oh, I just love it," gushed Cynthia.

Noelle rolled her eyes. Someone had to tell her that her husband was a scoundrel. It was all good and well for her; *she'd* had no idea that the man was married. This woman —she gazed at the jolly black feather perched on the top of Margaret's head— clearly knew that Kenneth was married. How could she not? She was evidently friends with his wife.

"Why don't you sit over there by the window," Cynthia was saying. "The lunch rush will be over soon and then we can have a little chat."

Margaret paid for her lunch and moved off to sit where Cynthia had indicated. Noelle's narrowed eyes followed her with distaste.

There were now only a handful of people between Noelle and the counter. Tiny little Cynthia was moving as fast as she could.

Noelle moved forward and then at last it was her turn. She smiled at Cynthia, trying not to betray a flicker of unease.

"Miss Brittler," squeaked Mrs. Black. She darted a quick glance around at her friend, who was still perched by the window. "I suppose you'd like to see Kenneth," she said in an undertone. "He just ran out. Would you like to wait?"

Noelle stared at the woman. What was going on? "I'm here to purchase a cake," she said calmly, raising an eyebrow. "I assume I can do that through you as well as Mr. Black?"

Cynthia looked taken aback. "Yes, of course, Miss," she said. "I've a book of sketches over here. Would you care to take a look?"

"That would be wonderful, thank you." Noelle sat down at the little barstool beside the counter and glanced behind her. The rush had dwindled down. There was now only two more customers in the shop apart from this Margaret and herself.

"Here you are," said Cynthia, pulling a small booklet out from under the counter. You let me know which you like and then..." she set down another piece of paper beside the booklet. "Here are our flavor options. I'll just finish with these gentlemen and I'll be right back over here."

Noelle smiled. She couldn't help it. Everything about poor little Cynthia was inviting and warm. How could any man want anything more than her? And what had she meant in assuming that Noelle was here to see Kenneth? Confusion tumbled and swirled around in her mind as she attempted to focus on the many drawings of immaculate cakes in front of her.

The little bell tinkled. A young woman entered, a small boy hanging onto her hand. Noelle went back to flipping through the booklet. She was dawdling. She knew perfectly well that her mother would flip to the back of the book and order whichever cake was the biggest and most expensive. The party that they were planning for her mother's 50th birthday was promising to be fantastic, and fantastically crowded. They might as well be planning a wedding for the queen herself.

But she was spinning out her time. Hoping, in the back of her mind, that Kenneth would return. That he might not flirt with her, and he might not prove to be the horrid individual that she knew he was. That way, she could at least admire him without detesting him. She wanted to believe that a man like Kenneth would be good to his wife; she wanted to envy Cynthia rather than pity her.

"How are you getting on?" Noelle jumped as Cynthia danced over to her, having just finished with the last customer. The little boy and his mother were now sitting at the only available table, and he was munching on a sugared biscuit.

"Fine, thank you," said Noelle. "I can't quite decide between your dark chocolate cherry display or your vanilla bean and apples."

Cynthia clucked her tongue sympathetically. "Both good choices," she said. "Although, I have to say that the dark chocolate cherry is one of our best sellers."

"Do you have anything with raspberries in it?" asked Noelle, flipping over the flavor menu to gaze at the back.

"Not generally," said Cynthia. Our raspberries are a little later in the season normally. Sometime around June."

"Out of curiosity," said Noelle, glancing up as someone passed by the bakery window. "Which of you normally does the cakes? Is it you? Or your husband?"

Cynthia's eyebrows shot up, and she giggled. Noelle couldn't see what was funny about the question.

"Oh, Miss Brittler, Kenneth isn't my—." She was cut off as the door chimed again and Kenneth Black stepped into the shop. "Ah, here he is," she said cheerfully.

Kenneth's arms were loaded with sacks of flour and sugar. "I can't believe we ran out," he was saying as he entered. "I thought for sure we'd ordered enough this t—." He froze, and his eyes widened as he spotted Noelle. One of the sacks of sugar hit the floor with a heavy thud. "Miss Brittler," he said. His voice had gone low and deep. "It's a pleasure to see you again."

"Mr. Black," said Noelle. She nodded at him and then turned back to Cynthia who was grinning.

"I think I'll leave Kenneth to help you with this one, my dear," said Cynthia, wrapping Noelle affectionately on the knuckles. And she walked away from Noelle, chuckling a little.

Flummoxed, Noelle watched Cynthia pour herself a glass of water and join her friend at the window. The woman called Margaret was watching Noelle with the same narrowed-eyed look Noelle had been giving her a few moments before. When Noelle looked at her, she nodded coldly and turned away.

"Well, Miss Brittler," said Kenneth, stooping to retrieve the sack he had dropped. "What can I do for you today? Not lost again, are you?"

Noelle raised her eyebrow at him. "I was never lost in the first place, Mr. Black," she said firmly. "I came to order the cake that you promised me."

Kenneth laughed and out of the corner of her eye, she saw Margaret casting her a dark look. Noelle fixed him with her furious stare, the one that she had practiced in the mirror. She had never felt so much like her mother's daughter in all her life.

The laughter drained from Kenneth's face. He frowned. "I don't recall promising anything to you, Miss," he said. "There was a sweet, friendly woman whom I think intended to order a cake from my bakery, but..." he looked her up and down deliberately, his eyes lingering and making her blush. Really. He was so forward... and right here. In front of his wife... and this other woman that was who-knew-what. Or... *was* Cynthia his wife? What had she been about to say to Noelle before Kenneth had come in...?

Kenneth shrugged and began taking things out of the sacks he'd set on the counter.

Noelle crossed her arms over her chest. She was warm. Her face was flushed, and she was entirely fed up with being confused. What did it really matter if Kenneth Black was married or not? What did it matter to her at least?

She could not have him even if he was available; her family would never stand for it.

"Mr. Black," she started, getting to her feet. "I would like to order a cake from your bakery."

She was very aware of his eyes when he turned around. Green, so green, and with the ability to make her tingle all over. It made her absolutely furious. "I think, in the end," sighed Kenneth, smiling a little sadly, "I shall make your cake. So, I suppose there is little point in arguing the matter. But..." he held up a finger, "I have a condition."

Noelle frowned at him. "What do you want?"

"You have to help me make it," said Kenneth. He was grinning again.

"Couldn't your wife do that for you?" growled Noelle, glancing over to the place where Cynthia sat, now engrossed in a whispered conversation with her friend. "Honestly," she said, very annoyed now. "You're not even remotely discrete with your..." she frowned... "indiscretions."

Kenneth was staring at her. "My indiscretions?" he asked, and he looked completely þaffled. "My wife? Miss Brittler, I am not married. Nor have I ever been."

Chapter Five

At last. A resolution. A reason for her behavior and her irrational irritation with him. “What gave you that impression?” he asked, trying his very hardest not to laugh. Of all the stupid... Why hadn’t he thought of that?

Noelle was looking at him, and her eyes were wide. “But... Cynthia... Oh.” A look of dawning comprehension slid over Noelle’s sweet face, and her cheeks darkened to crimson. “I thought...” she trailed off for a moment, biting her lip, and Kenneth was visited by a strong urge to bite her lip as well. “You have the same last name.” She indicated Cynthia, sitting in the corner with Margaret, who kept throwing daggers in his direction with her eyes. “You and Cynthia,” she sighed, her body deflating, and Kenneth watched her furious demeanor melt away. “She’s your sister, isn’t she?” she finished finally.

It wasn't really a question, but he answered it with fervor. "Yes," he said. And he laughed then, relief pounding through his head in a wave so strong it almost made him dizzy. "She's my sister. From birth, regrettably." Cynthia cast a glare in his direction and he winked at her.

"So," said Noelle, slumping forward on the barstool. "You're not a despicable human being?"

Kenneth laughed again. He couldn't seem to stop. Something about this woman reached out to him on a level he'd long since forgotten. "Well, I'll not go quite as far as that," he said. "Believe me, I can be quite despicable when I want to be." He let his eyes slide over her fine form once more. That was another thing he couldn't seem to help. It was going to get him into trouble. But that dress. It was falling off her shoulder just so. She looked remarkable.

And she was still blushing. "I don't doubt that at all," she said. "Very well, Mr. Black. I will assist in the baking of my mother's birthday cake. But I will expect a very fine discount if that is the case."

"Certainly not," chuckled Kenneth. "Deals off."

"Oh come, come, don't be silly." She was rapidly recovering from her embarrassment. "If I'm required to assist, it's only fair."

"Oh, we'll see if we can't work something out," he said, smiling wickedly. "When do you need it by?"

She brushed a strand of long, golden hair out of her eyes and wiggled a bit on the stool as she thought. "Her birthday is the week after next. My aunt has thrown together a massive party," he watched her roll her eyes to the ceiling. "It should be the party of the century."

"I'm sure it will be," said Kenneth. "If the Brittlers are hosting it," he smiled, meaning it as a compliment, but he could tell that Noelle did not take it as such. Her face fell slightly, as though she assumed he meant to emphasize the stark contrast of their stations. "I only meant," he said hurriedly. Heaven help him if she ran away from him again. "That your family's parties are renowned."

Noelle smiled. "I think they're positively ridiculous, and I'm sure you do too. It's alright to say it you know."

He grinned at her. "They're a bit..." he paused, searching for the word. "Vast," he said finally, doing his very best not to insult her.

Words often tumbled out of his mouth before he had a chance to wrap his mind around them, but what good was it to walk on eggshells around everyone you met? He wasn't one to put on a show. He was straight-forward, nothing hidden behind the curtain, and he was also in luck.

She giggled. Very prettily too. "Vast," she said thoughtfully. "Yes. I suppose they are rather vast."

He shrugged. "I can't imagine it being very fun," he said, again without thinking. "Everyone in their stuffy suits and drinking champagne while they nibble on tiny desserts. I don't know... Maybe it's more entertaining than it sounds like it will be."

Noelle frowned at him. "They're not all bad," she said. "At my birthday last year, I danced all night. I do like dancing, you know."

"I'd imagine that you do," said Kenneth. He imagined her out on a dance floor in his arms. Perhaps they would waltz. Perhaps the room would be bathed in gold candlelight. "I suppose it can't be all that bad," he acknowledged with a grin.

She was looking at him. "Mr. Black, I would like to make an amendment to our agreement."

"Oh?"

Her warm, inviting lips had quirked up mischievously. "I will help you bake a cake, if you attend my Mother's birthday celebration with me."

He laughed. He was sure that she was joking. When she remained stubbornly sober, he stared at her. "I'd never be allowed in!" he exclaimed.

"Let's see," said Noelle. She stood up and came around the counter. He liked the casual way she approached him, her pink dress swaying like a bell around her hips. She came right up next to him so that the soft fabric engulfed his ankles, then she tugged at his collar and straightened his hair. "Yes," she said. "I think you could certainly pass as some visiting nobleman or other.

"Oh, really?" he said sarcastically.

"Why not?" she whispered excitedly. "Oh, please come. It would give me something to look forward to."

"It's in two weeks?" he asked. "And, isn't it a house party? How long do you think we could keep up the charade? Someone is bound to notice something amiss over the course of an entire weekend. If it were one night, it would be different..."

"I'll secure you an invitation," she said excitedly, clapping her hands.

"Noelle, I can't! Someone will recognize me."

"Tosh," she said, and she swooped back around the counter to gather her handbag. "I'll see you next week. What time should I come to the bakery?"

"Err," he was feeling a little dumbstruck. "In the morning?"

She giggled. "Friday morning?"

"Thursday," he said, shaking his head experimentally, like a dog trying to rid its ears of water. "We'll need to—."

"Wonderful," she said still bubbling with enthusiasm. "I'll see you on Thursday morning."

As Noelle Brittler sashayed out the door, he watched her go with his eyes wide, rubbing the short bristles on the back of his neck. What had he gotten himself into?

"Who was that?"

Confound it all.

"Her name is Noelle," he said, turning to survey Margaret Piper as she sidled up to him, a coy smile on her face.

"Brittler?" asked Margaret, tapping her chin, a rather knowing smile mushing its way onto her pallid face.

"Yes, that's her," he said. He turned away from Margaret's eager expression. He had no wish to deal with her advances this afternoon.

She followed him down the counter, meeting him on the other end. "The Brittlers are rather interesting," she said, fixing him with her small, dark eyes. "But I'm afraid us commoners are nothing more than a way for them to pass the time," she tugged on his shirt sleeve to get his attention as he attempted to fill a jar with flour and some of it scattered onto the counter top. He glared at her.

"I think I'd like to form my own opinions, thank you very much," he said grumpily. A moment ago, he had been floating on air. Now he was stuck crossing swords with Margaret Piper, who could not hold her tongue to save her life, and he was not at all in the mood to do so. He reached under the counter to retrieve a damp rag to mop up the mess she'd made.

"Suit yourself," said Margaret. "Don't say I didn't warn you though." She turned away from him, and Kenneth breathed a sigh of relief. "I'd better get back to the shop," she said, swinging her hips as she walked away from him. He tried not to laugh out loud as she nearly toppled over a stool. "Are you still planning on dropping by the shop tomorrow, Cynthia?"

His sister had been watching him interact with Margaret with a look of utter and complete amusement on her face. "Yes, I think so. Perhaps I can talk Kenneth into joining me. From what I overheard, he's going to be in need of a new suit in a few weeks' time."

Kenneth threw the towel at her.

"This is a bad idea." Kenneth was staring down at himself in a tall mirror at the tailor's shop the following Sunday. "I can't possibly go through with this."

He heard Cynthia hiss from behind the rows of fabric on the other side of the store.

Noelle had been as good as her word. The following day, a letter had arrived in the post. It had been hand-written in a great hurry.

Dear Mr. Black,

Everything is set. I have secured an invitation for you under the pretense that you are a well-known architect from Ireland whom I happened to meet while I was out shopping just yesterday. We'll hammer out the finer details when I see you on Thursday.

Hoping you are well,

Noelle Brittler

"This is bad. Very bad. I can't believe you're making me do this." He glared at his sister in the mirror as she rounded the shelves and came to stand beside him.

She grinned. "You, my dear brother, have somehow managed to get your hands on an invitation to one of the most cultivated events in Manhattan. You simply must go," she said firmly.

"If I get caught..."

"Honestly, Ken, what's the worst that could happen?"

"If I get caught, I'll be a laughing stock.

"If you get caught it will mean loads of free publicity for the bakery. Think, Ken. We might make the society newspapers!"

He folded his arms over his chest and frowned down at Cynthia, who was a foot shorter than she usually was because he was standing on a raised box. "I don't want to be in the society papers," he said, his voice as sour as buttermilk. "We're doing fine on our own."

Cynthia snorted. "Then why haven't we hired on a few helping hands?"

"We're doing fine on our own," Kenneth repeated.

The tailor stepped back into the room and knelt down beside Kenneth's feet, seemingly oblivious to the steam issuing from his client's nostrils. "Let's see. We'll raise the hem here, and perhaps pull the suit in right up here. It doesn't need much else Mr. Black, this is the largest size that I keep on hand in the shop."

Kenneth glanced at himself in the mirror for a final time, feeling every inch the fool, then he gave the tailor a sharp nod and stepped off the crate.

"When will it be ready?" he asked, tugging off the tail-coat.

"Oh, I'd say I could have it finished up around Tuesday," said the tailor with a smile. "Will you be needing anything else?"

As Kenneth shook his head, Cynthia stepped forward. "He'll be needing a new pair of shoes and a tie. And possibly a few casual dress shirts."

"What's the matter with the shoes I already have?"

Cynthia did not deign to respond.

Kenneth slunk away into the back room to change and tried to ignore the dull ache that was forming behind his eyes. He hadn't slept much the night before. His tumbling thoughts had kept him awake late into the night, torn between excitement and anxiety.

It wasn't as though he wasn't a brave man. Kenneth was never one to shy away from confrontation. No, his main concern was that he couldn't see any sense in Miss Noelle Brittler's plans for him. What good would it do to parade him in front of all of Manhattan's high society? It would stir up questions and intrigue, and most likely get them both into trouble. And then he thought of the way her eyes had lit up with enthusiasm as the idea had struck her. She had looked like a child at Christmas. Her pretty cheeks had flushed...

"Sir, do you need help with the pins?"

Kenneth gave a guilty start.

"I'm alright, thank you," he responded through the door. He heard the heavy footfalls of the tailor moving back into the front room and sighed.

His gaze found a tall mirror in the corner and he avoided his own eyes. This was the sort of thing that he had always striven to avoid. Disturbance in his otherwise peaceful existence. And here he was, being coerced into yet another situation that would test his limits.

Admittedly, he had not fought very hard against Noelle's playful banter. He'd only met the woman a matter of days ago and already she seemed to occupy his every waking thought—and a many of his sleeping ones as well. Kenneth felt his ears turn red as he recalled the dream he had had the night before. He hardly knew the woman; if she were to suddenly develop the capabilities required to see inside his head, he would be in some very hot water indeed.

He and Cynthia exited the tailor's shop laden with packages and several long receipts that dictated when Kenneth was supposed to return to pick up his order. As they crossed the narrow street, heading for the bakery, he caught sight of something that made his breath catch in his chest. He stopped in his tracks, staring, and Cynthia walked right into him.

"What the devil, Ken?" she snapped as she bent low to retrieve her fallen parcels.

Normally, he would have chastised his sister for her lack of manners, but he was too busy peering over the heads of the crowd to try and catch sight of the face he had glimpsed. It couldn't be.

Cynthia was straightening up. "What is it?" she asked, having caught sight of his face.

"That man," he said, his eyes still scanning the crowd.

"What man?" Cynthia was standing on her tiptoes, trying to see what had distracted him.

"He should be sitting on his duff in the jailhouse," said Kenneth under his breath.

"Ken," Cynthia had taken hold of his shirt sleeve. "You're not making any sense."

Kenneth looked down and found his sister's anxious face peering up into his. "I'm sure I just saw Jeb Dillard. The man who attacked Noelle last week. He was watching us from just over there," he indicated the front of the nearby post office."

"I thought you said they took him to the constable," said Cynthia.

"They did."

"Then he's escaped?"

Kenneth's eyes had flown back to the people around them. "Maybe," he said.

"Well, what's it matter if he has escaped?" whispered Cynthia. "He's ruined now, with a black mark like that. Once word gets out, he'll have a job finding work."

"And who do you think he'll blame for that?" hissed Kenneth. He glared down at Cynthia and watched her eyes widen.

"You?" she said, aghast.

"I'd bet a batch of biscuits on it," said Kenneth. He hefted his packages more securely into his arms and motioned Cynthia forward. "Come on. If Dillard is on the lookout for me I don't want to make it too easy for him."

"Are you sure you aren't just being paranoid?"

Kenneth frowned, but didn't answer. No, he wasn't sure, but he'd rather be safe than sorry.

He led his sister around the corner and away from the hustle of the main street.

"Where are we going?"

"On a merry chase," said Kenneth under his breath. "Don't look back," he added as Cynthia glanced over her shoulder. "Don't let him know he's been made."

They proceeded down the next street and turned a corner at random, zig-zagging a path through the busy Manhattan avenues.

At an intersection, Kenneth paused, glancing conspicuously into the mirrored reflection in the department store window across the street. At first, he thought perhaps that he had been imagining things. Then, several yards away from where they stood, he noticed a familiar hulking figure, a bowler hat pulled low over his eyes to shield his face.

Kenneth let out a low grunt of satisfaction. "Let's go," he said, and he took hold of Cynthia's arm once more.

They wove through the crowd to the department store and slid inside. "What are you doing?" his sister hissed, "Let's keep moving."

"If we run, he'll know we know he's following," said Kenneth, tucking Cynthia's arm into the crook of his elbow and smiling at a small family as they passed them. "We need to appear as though we haven't noticed him."

Cynthia glared at him. "I can't believe this. Why is he following us? What could he have to gain by skulking around?"

"He's trying to catch me off-guard. He knows I think he's still under lock and key. I think he wants to learn my routines. Discover who I might be close to…" he trailed off as his sister's eyes widened. "Yes."

Kenneth steered them through the aisles, pretending to be looking at the different items on display in case Jeb Dillard happened to be peering in through a window, and Cynthia followed his lead.

"All of this for the sake of that Brittler girl?" she whispered out of the corner of her mouth, bending to lift a hat from a low shelf.

"What was I supposed to do, Cynthia? I couldn't very well just continue on my way while she screamed."

His sister said nothing, and he knew it was because she couldn't think of anything to say that wouldn't sound heartless.

They toured the shop for a few more minutes and then Cynthia approached the counter and purchased a velvet hair bow.

"What?" she asked when Kenneth raised his eyebrows at her. "If we don't buy anything, it will look suspicious."

Rolling his eyes at her, Kenneth stepped out into the street and peered around. He couldn't see Dillard, but that didn't mean that the man wasn't lurking around a corner somewhere.

"I don't want to lead him straight to the shop," he said when Cynthia reappeared next to him. "We'll see if we can lose him in the mercantile."

She nodded and they set off.

Chapter Six

Noelle was in the kitchen and her heart was pounding rather fast, considering all that she was doing was twirling a wooden spoon around a mixing bowl.

"A little faster, dear," Marcia was saying to her. "You need to beat out all the lumps."

Some of the dry cake mix tumbled out of the bowl and onto the counter as Noelle did as she was told. It was Wednesday afternoon, and Noelle had asked their cook to show her a few tips before she went to help Kenneth Black the following morning. She didn't want to appear completely negligent in the area. She was a good baker, something that her mother generally encouraged her to hide from the public, but her expertise revolved around bread making. Even so, she had never made anything like what she had tasted the other night at La Petite Paradis.

"Why the sudden interest in cakes?" asked Marcia. She was eyeing Noelle suspiciously, and Noelle knew that she had blushed.

"I'm just..." she hesitated with the Cook's eyes boring into her like daggers. "Attempting to expand my horizons," she said. "I'm getting rather good at the breads now."

To her relief, Marcia smiled. "Yes, you are," she said turning back to the sink.

Noelle sighed and went back to her mixing. Unfortunately for her, the Brittlers' family cook was an uncommonly observant woman. Her eyes were sharp and her manner was strict and off-putting, but Noelle had managed to gain favor in Marcia's eyes through her interest in the culinary arts.

"So, what comes next?" she asked, turning her head so that she could peer at the open recipe book beside her.

"Get your butter out of the icebox," said Marcia, "it'll need to soften up first."

As Noelle moved across the kitchen, an echoing crack sounded in the hall. The butter dish slipped through her fingers and Marcia shrieked. "Great heavens above! What was that?"

They looked at one another.

"Who's there?" Marcia called out. "Kincaid? Is that you?"

When no answer came, Marcia turned a puzzled expression to Noelle. "Your parents are still at the Gerson's for the day?"

Noelle nodded. Together, the two women poked their heads around the kitchen door. Nothing appeared to be out of place.

"What was that?"

Noelle peered left and right and then stepped cautiously through the doorway. "There's nothing here at all."

"Did a frame fall off the wall?"

She examined the paintings that lined the hallway. Nothing. She shrugged. "Should we call someone?"

Marcia frowned around. "If I was superstitious, I'd say your granny had come back to pay ye a visit and let ya know she's quite displeased."

Noelle laughed. "Marcia, darling, if Granny comes back to see me, she won't be satisfied with a mere rattle or shake. That woman would sit on the end of my bed in the dead of night and lecture me for hours. I wouldn't get a wink of sleep."

Marcia let out a throaty croak of laughter. "That does sound more like her. You remember when she traveled all the way from London just to tell your mother how displeased she was with your cousin?"

"How could I forget? She went on about him for days on end. She hardly drew breath, Lord rest her soul."

Laughing, Marcia wandered back into the kitchen and returned to her task.

Noelle peered around the hall, looking for the source of the noise. She was about to turn back into the kitchen when she saw it. The window on the far wall was cracked. She stared at the broken pane. Had a bird flown into the glass?

She bent to examine it and the afternoon sunlight glanced off something sitting in the bush just below the window outside, as if it had been thrown. Before opening it, she glanced around into the garden, but the yard was empty.

Mentally shaking herself, Noelle slid the catch and heaved the frame open, reaching for the round, dark something she could make out through the leaves. When at last she grasped it, she discovered it was a rock wrapped in brown paper. Curious, she undid the wrappings and unfolded the parchment.

Written in a sloppy hand, were four lopsided words:

FOUND YOU PRETTY GIRL

The rock fell from her hand and rolled across the floor with a clatter. She stared at the scribbled black words in front of her, transfixed. Then she slammed the window shut and locked it.

Her hands were shaking. It was a prank, it had to be. Someone was trying to scare her. Why though?

With a rush of loathing, she remembered the last words that her would-be attacker had screamed at her before he was hauled away to the constable.

"You ain't seen the last of me," he had said.

What should she do?

"Everything alright out there, love?" Marcia called from the kitchen.

"It's fine," Noelle croaked. She crumpled the missive in her fist, her mind working furiously.

She hadn't told anyone in her family what had happened to her the day she went to town for mother's cake. If she had told her father, Kincaid would have lost his job. IF she had told her mother, she would have told her father. Her one hour of distress was not worth costing a good man his livelihood. Nothing had truly happened to her.

She had been saved and her attacker had gone to prison. Or... so she thought.

Was she in danger? Noelle glanced out the window one more time.

Think, she told herself. *Think. What would Dianna do?*

She couldn't go to her parents. She couldn't go to their butler and head of the household staff. Noelle exhaled slowly, her fingers at her temples as she thought, and then it came to her. She would tell Kincaid himself and trust his desire to remain employed as insurance that he would protect her at all costs.

Her shoulders relaxed. Kincaid was a good man. He would keep her safe.

And she *had* broken Jeb's nose the last time they had met. Surely, she was at least somewhat capable of defending herself.

She thought briefly about telling Kenneth Black, but strangely, she didn't like the idea of tainting their easy relationship with worry. He would make a fuss. He might urge her to tell her parents or go to the police, and Noelle did not want either of those things. The story was embarrassing enough without having to relay it several times over and create a massive scandal. She could see the headlines now.

No. It was her mother's 50th birthday. She wasn't going to bring that mess down onto her family's head.

Despite her best efforts to calm herself, when darkness crept over the Brittler Family Estate, Noelle found herself growing edgy. She peered into shadows along the hall and through open doors as she made her way to bed.

Later, lying awake and staring at the canopy over her head, she found herself shivering. The night was warm, and she could just make out the sound of crickets chirping cheerfully outside her bedroom window. Inexplicably, she thought of Kenneth. The memory of his smile made her feel safe. She drifted off at last thinking about the coming day.

Noelle awoke the following morning to the smell of something sweet. It took her several sleepy moments before she realized that her fingers still smelled of cake from the day before. For a minute, she lay there, unwilling to let herself come fully awake.

She had dreamed of warm wheat bread and a glittering fire. There had been someone else there too. Someone tall, and as warm as the flames themselves. His laugh had been intoxicating, and his smile intriguing, and his hands had been...

Noelle's eyes flew open, her fingers flying to her mouth in embarrassment, although no one was around to see. She lay in bed for as long as she dared, her heart hammering out a crazy rhythm against her breastbone.

And as she rose from her bed and started to get dressed, her thoughts were all of Kenneth Black, and whether or not his kisses would really taste like chocolate cake.

"It's about time you showed up!" Kenneth hardly glanced up from what he was doing as Noelle hurried in through the bakery door, her smile sheepish.

"I'm sorry! I didn't mean to arrive so late, I'm not sure where the time went this morning." Kincaid had insisted —after their rather serious conversation that morning— that they take a round-about path to the bakery, so that he could be sure they weren't followed. Once they had arrived, Kenneth had insisted on scouting the surrounding area before allowing Noelle out of the carriage. Even as she spoke, her footman had parked himself beside the front door, standing to attention like a soldier. She had managed to talk him out of going to the police, insisting this Jeb character wasn't even worth the trouble. All she asked was that he kept a weathered eye out for anything suspicious.

"It's hardly morning anymore," grumbled Kenneth, but he smiled when he finally looked up at her. "We'd better get started."

Cynthia was helping the first customers of the day, and Noelle noticed that she looked harried and irritable, returning Noelle's smile only half-heartedly as she danced around behind the counter.

"Come into the back," Kenneth called, and Noelle hastened to follow him through a long curtain that she hadn't noticed during her first few visits. It led to a large kitchen, though in truth, the room more resembled a workshop than a kitchen. Various implements for stirring, whisking, crushing and slicing were hung on the far wall, spaced so evenly, that for a moment Noelle was reminded of the garden shed on her family's estate. She'd never thought of a kitchen as a workplace before, but it was clear from a glance that Kenneth treated it as such.

She didn't have much time to look around, however, because a moment later, Kenneth had tossed a starched cotton apron into her face.

"Come on, no time to stand around," he winked at her and beckoned her over to him. Noelle came, tying the apron strings behind her back.

She tried not to stare at his hands as he riffled through a recipe book, but the previous nights' dream kept invading her thoughts like a conquering army and she could tell the color was high in her cheeks, because Kenneth continued to glance up at her periodically.

But he was all business. There was little of the easy flirtation they had been enjoying. He was in his element.

"Here," he said, shifting around a large cutting table in the center of the room so that he could show Noelle the recipe book. "Take a look at this. See? Now this," he held up a bundle of measuring spoons, "is a *teaspoon*," he announced slowly, as though Noelle was a bit dim. "You use it to measure out ingredients."

Noelle chose to play along. "Is that so?" she asked. She took the measuring spoons and proceeded to examine them as if she'd never seen anything so interesting in all her life and then, spotting a knife on the table before her: "So you would use this to chop the dough!" she said, lifting it and staring at Kenneth expectantly with an expression of complete innocence on her face.

Kenneth chuckled and Noelle was a little offended to see that he thought she was serious.

"No, no, no," he said taking the knife from her and replacing it on the cutting table. Noelle raised her eyebrows at him, but he didn't seem to notice. When he looked at her again, Noelle screwed up her face as though she were having difficulty understanding.

"Interesting," she said her voice heavy with sarcasm. "Alright, shall we get started then?"

Kenneth's green eyes widened as though he was taken aback. "I thought you might want me to take you through it slowly," he said.

"Mr. Black, I can assure you that the function of each and every utensil on this table does not escape me, except perhaps that one," she said, indicating a strange shaped silver instrument with a bouncing coil on either end.

"Uhh...right," muttered Kenneth, and Noelle was pleased to see that he had stopped looking haughty and all-knowing. The back of his neck had reddened a bit.

"Right," he said again, toying with his apron string.

"Can I have a look at the book?"

"Help yourself," muttered Kenneth. His nose was still a bit pink. He slid the recipe book across the table without looking at her and then sat down on a spindly legged stool. "Let me know if you have any questions."

Noelle felt her lips quirk into a forgiving smile. She ran her finger down the list of ingredients, looking around the kitchen in search of them as she did so. Kenneth sat in an embarrassed silence, all of his self-assurance vanishing like a candle being snuffed out in an unexpected breeze.

Noelle located the flour and sugar in large, labeled canisters on the opposite wall and carried them over to the cutting table. Now apparently taking his lead from her, Kenneth stood and began strolling around the shelves, pulling out ingredients.

"I didn't mean to," he started, still not looking at her as he set a jar of cocoa down on the cutting table. "It's just a bit uncommon for someone of your..."

"Birth? Class?" Noelle fixed a frown on her face as she began spooning each of the dry ingredients into a mixing bowl. "Not all of us spend our time sewing and attending societal functions, Mr. Black. And..." she dipped a tiny quarter teaspoon into the cocoa powder. "I think you would be very surprised to learn that many of us are aware of the function of a teaspoon." Grinning, she pulled the tiny spoon back and launched the cocoa powder onto the front of Kenneth's apron.

Shock flickered across his handsome features and then he laughed, brushing at the dark spot with one of his magnificent hands. “Is that so?” He was still chuckling. He dipped a finger into the sugar and came around the corner of the cutting table. “Aren’t you just full of surprises?”

“Stay back, you,” Noelle giggled. She reached out and seized a wooden spoon in her fist, fending him off.

“What, Miss Brittler? You’re not afraid of a bit of sugar, are you?”

Noelle shrieked as he lunged at her. “It’s not the sugar that frightens me, sir!”

Giggling, she darted around the table and dipped her fingers into the butter dish. “Don’t you come any closer!”

“Oh, Miss Brittler,” said Kenneth, his chest vibrating with silent laughter. “You play dirty.”

“And rightly so. Look at the size of you. In a fair fight, you’d crush me!” She blushed then, having spoken without thinking, and she could tell his mind had strayed at the idea of his body crushing against hers. His expression darkened suggestively.

What was she doing?

“I’ll concede if you do,” he said suddenly, straightening from his half-crouched position, a seductive, crooked grin playing around his lips.

"Agreed," said Noelle, her shoulders relaxing. She reached for a tea towel to wipe the butter from her fingertips, but all at once, Kenneth lunged at her, and in a second, her nose and lips were dotted with flecks of sugar.

"You're a cheat!" She laughed, scrubbing at her flushed cheeks.

Kenneth's laugh was deep and appreciative. "I said I would concede," he chuckled. "I didn't say when."

Shaking her head, Noelle used the tea towel in her hand to dust the fine grains of sugar away from her lips.

"Here," muttered Kenneth. He was watching her struggle with a self-satisfied look on his face. He took the towel from her and brushed it over the tip of her nose, lifting her chin in his other hand.

He was quite focused on his task, his dark brow furrowed and his eyes intent. Noelle was startled at the ease of his closeness. It felt warm and easy, and suddenly intimate.

He was at least a foot taller than her. She could smell the rich, masculine scent coming from his skin. He was freshly shaven, and he smelled of soap, and something decidedly Kenneth. Quirky, unusual, and sweet. He was warm and his eyes were deep and dark, and so green. Noelle thought she could lose herself in them. Then he looked at her, and he seemed to become aware of their proximity.

Noelle felt his fingers twitch against her jaw, as though he'd started to pull away from her and then thought better of it. His green eyes were dancing over her face like the wings of a butterfly. She could feel each place they landed. Her eyes, her cheeks... her lips.

His fingers, so gentle as they held her chin, were abruptly guiding her face closer to his, and she could feel his breath mingling with her own. Was he going to kiss her? Should she let him kiss her?

There was a clatter from the front room and both of them jumped, a second later, Cynthia's tiny dark head was peering through the curtain. Noelle took a hasty step back, her fingers flying to her waist, instinctively straightening her skirts as she did whenever her mother happened to enter a room.

"Kenneth," Cynthia growled. "I could use a hand!"

Kenneth frowned at his sister. "I'll be there in a minute," he said. He turned puzzled eyes onto Noelle and opened his mouth.

"Kenneth, please!" Cynthia begged. "It's mayhem out here."

Grumbling under his breath, Kenneth cast Noelle an apologetic look before heading toward the curtained doorway. Cynthia lingered a moment longer, glaring suspiciously between Noelle and her brother, then she withdrew and Kenneth followed her.

Noelle sagged into the counter top, her heart pounding rather harder than it should be. Her mind was whirling.

No, she told herself, *no. He's off limits. Just as much as he was when you thought he was married. There is no future there...How can there be?* But even as she thought it, Noelle saw herself here. Maybe her hands would be busily kneading bread dough. Perhaps Kenneth would come in and nibble on her ear. Then, maybe one day, there would be a child holding on to her skirts. A child with brilliantly green eyes.

Lost in the happy, impossible future her imagination was conjuring, Noelle turned her eyes back to the recipe book and started in on the cake. As she began to measure out the ingredients, she idly brushed away the last traces of sugar from her lips, and when she tasted them, they were sweet.

It was some time before Kenneth reappeared in the kitchen. When he did, Noelle noticed he had removed his vest and rolled up his shirt sleeves. It was the first time she had gotten a good look at his arms, which were lean and muscular and covered in a fine dusting of soft hair and freckles. When Kenneth cleared his throat, Noelle flushed and realized she'd been staring.

"The cake's nearly out," she said, turning to the small wood-fired oven in the corner of the room.

"You've... you've finished it?"

"Well, I wouldn't say that," she said with a sheepish grin. "You'll need to have a look at it to see how I've done."

Kenneth sauntered over to the oven, looking impressed. "How long has it been in there?" He asked, bending at the waist and pulling open the oven door.

"About twenty minutes?" He nodded approvingly, and Noelle let out a little humph of satisfaction. "You didn't think I could do it, did you?" She smirked.

Kenneth held up his hands in a gesture as if to say: 'I had my doubts.'

Noelle threw the tea towel at him.

Grinning, Kenneth caught it and tossed it back at her. "Come sit down and have lunch with us. We should have a little break in customers about now. It's nearly two."

Noelle followed him out into the front room, and was somehow surprised to see Cynthia there, handing a final bun across the counter to an elderly gentleman in a green tweed coat and matching hat.

"That'll be all for you Mr. Davies? Won't you be wanting your iced scones?"

Mr. Davies chuckled and patted his belly. "Thanks, but no, sweetheart. The Missus has been on me about the state of the buttons on my waistcoat."

Cynthia's laugh was charming. "You look as handsome as ever Mr. Davies. I'll be seeing you tomorrow then?"

"Naturally," he said. He offered Cynthia a crooked-toothed grin and, doffing his hat to Kenneth and Noelle, he made his slow progress out the front door.

Cynthia followed after him and spun the sign on the door from open to closed. "There," she said, smiling and looking marginally more cheerful than she had when Noelle had first arrived. "I think there's plenty of soup left. Shall we have that for lunch?"

They all crowded around the counter. Kenneth reached up above his head and lifted down three bowls. Noelle, remembering having spotted the silverware to the left of the icebox, went to retrieve it as Cynthia filled the bowls and laid out a savory scone for each of them.

"So, how did you do with the cake?" asked Cynthia as the three of them sat down around one of the tables, their bowls of soup steaming in the light from the windows.

"I suppose we won't know until it comes out of the oven," said Noelle, blowing on her spoon, "but I think I've done alright."

"Do you do much cooking up in that mansion of yours?" Cynthia's tone was light, but Kenneth said:

"Cynthia..." warningly, as though he was reminding her of something that the siblings had agreed upon before Noelle had arrived.

Noelle raised her eyebrows at them both. "Our cook, Marcia, she's been giving me lessons once or twice a week for several years now. Since just before my eldest sister was married."

Noelle didn't know why this news should be a revelation to them, but both Kenneth and Cynthia had exchanged looks full of hidden meaning.

"What?" asked Noelle, feeling a bit put off. This sort of behavior was the sort that she expected from her own family. Her aunt. Maybe a wealthy suitor or a friend of her mother's, but their reactions had left her feeling deflated. She had thought they would understand.

Kenneth scratched his nose uncomfortably. "We seemed to have formed a mistaken impression of you, Miss Brittler," he said, looking apologetic.

"You and everyone else in the world," Noelle scoffed. She fiddled with her spoon, no longer hungry.

"We didn't mean to offend you," said Cynthia hurriedly.

"Not at all, not at all. Not offended," said Noelle, forcing her disappointment to the back of her mind and smiling at the siblings. "I would think it is a common misconception to think that my family has little in the way of hobbies, as we're so restricted by the weather."

"The weather?" said Kenneth, a dark crease marring his brow.

"Yes," said Noelle. "The sunlight makes it very difficult for us to pursue our usual habits of hunting innocent victims and draining them of their blood."

Kenneth spat out his mouthful of soup and Cynthia thumped him on the back while she let out a high, tinkling laugh.

Smirking, Noelle said: "I feel it's important for everyone to have a skill. The best part of my chosen line of study is that I get to eat my projects once I've finished them."

Kenneth had sat back in his chair with his arms folded, looking as though he daren't take another bite of soup until he was sure that Noelle was finished speaking. When she had he said:

"It's a good skill to hone," approvingly, and Noelle could tell he was impressed with her.

"I thought you would approve," she smirked again and returned to her soup.

Chapter Seven

Why did she have to smile like that? She looked at him as though she were enjoying some private joke, and he longed to know what it was. Confound it all! He wanted to know everything about her. Most of all, he wanted to return to that moment, the quiet, playful moment when she had been so close to him...

Her dazzling blue eyes met his over her spoon and she raised her eyebrows inquiringly. Out of the corner of his eye, his noticed Cynthia's eyes on him as well and he realized he must be staring. Swallowing, Kenneth attempted to redirect his gaze, taking a little longer than normal to make sense of Cynthia's next words.

"So, do any of your sisters share in your opinions? What is it that they like to do?"

Kenneth's eyes snapped back to Noelle as she shifted a bit in her seat, her eyes narrowing in thought.

"Well, Charlotte seems to have taken up painting alongside her husband in Colorado. They've opened a small gallery in their drawing room, apparently. She's sent a few pieces along to us and I think they're very good, but I'm rather biased. I'll show them to you," she said to him, nodding in his direction. "When you come up to the house next week."

"I'd love to see them," said Kenneth, clearing his throat.

Cynthia let out a bark of laughter. "Since when are you interested in art, Ken?" she chuckled.

"Since Miss Noelle has deigned to honor me with an invitation to see a bit of it," he responded, not looking at his sister. His eyes were busy memorizing the way Noelle's lit up when she smiled at him, and he wondered if she knew what sort of effect she was having on him.

"Oh no!"

Kenneth jumped as Noelle suddenly leapt to her feet.

"The cake!" she squawked.

He got to his feet quickly and followed her into the kitchen, Cynthia hot on his heels.

"Oh, no. I hope it's not burnt," Noelle was saying desperately as she scooped her skirts behind her and bent to open the oven. The smell hit him as it was flung open.

Warm and rich and perfect, yet somehow different than what he had been expecting. He couldn't detect the change. A spice? Perhaps?

Noelle was still bent double, her rump high in the air as she reached to retrieve her cake.

Kenneth swallowed.

When she straightened, Noelle's face was red and her cheeks were damp with the steam from the oven. She set the cake down on the counter gingerly and peered at it. "What do you think?" she asked Kenneth. He bent forward too. The kitchen was full of the scent of the cake.

"You used the recipe in the book, right?" he asked, prodding at the spongey top.

Noelle nodded and then paused. "Well, for the most part," she said.

"For the most part?" Kenneth looked at her and was amused to see that her grin was back in place, full of mischief.

"For the most part," she repeated, coyly. She darted back to the oven and removed two more cake plates, each one with its color slightly different than the first.

Cynthia was standing silently in the corner, her arms folded, her sharp eyes taking in every detail of the scene before her.

"What did you do to them?" Kenneth asked.

"Oh, a little of this, a little of that," said Noelle. She winked at him. Boldly, proudly.

"Oh, do tell," said Cynthia. She had come to stand beside Kenneth, and very briefly, he wished her away. He wanted this moment alone with Noelle. He wanted to cajole her, to tease her into telling him what she had done to his recipe. He wanted... What did he want? His thoughts were becoming muddled by the intoxicating scent of the cake, and by Noelle. But he was feeling trapped by his sister and her dire warnings. Just last night, they had argued.

"Tell her the truth, Kenneth," Cynthia had said. "There's a man out there that might wish you both harm. He lost his livelihood because you saved her from him. You said yourself you thought he would come after you, what makes you think that he'll stop there?"

"I can take care of this," Kenneth had said. "She doesn't need to know. It will only frighten her. Hasn't she endured enough?"

"Enough?" snapped Cynthia, pacing back and forth across the kitchen floor. "What exactly has she endured? A man's groping hands? Please."

"Why do you think so very little of her?"

At this, his sister had let out a derisive laugh. “All our lives,” she said, coming right up to him and planting herself down on the bar stool next to the cutting table. “We have bowed and scraped and saved and wallowed down here in the dirt. Fighting just to make do. Fighting alone. Just you and me. No one else. While she...” Cynthia closed her eyes as though she was willing herself to remain calm. “She has had everything handed to her on a silver platter.”

“There’s more to her than that,” said Kenneth. He placed a hand on Cynthia’s shoulder. “Truly.”

“I saw the way you’ve been looking at her,” she said. “It’ll do you more harm than good to get yourself all riled up for the likes of her. She’s so far above us she might as well be amongst the heavens themselves.”

“I think she feels something for me,” he said softly.

Cynthia seized a nearby wooden spoon and wrapped him smartly on the top of the head.

“Ouch! Cynthia!”

“You’ll go to this thing, this birthday celebration for her mum,” said Cynthia, glaring at him and brandishing the wooden spoon like a knife. “You’ll go, because you’ve given her your word, and because this is the chance of a lifetime, but once this is over, that’s it. Kenneth, you’ll have to let her go.”

"Why?" grumbled Kenneth, rubbing the top of his head.

"Because she's no good for you," said his sister, more quietly now. "She's a Brittler, Ken. She's the daughter of one of the wealthiest men in the country."

"But..."

"Say she does feel something for you. Just say she does. Think about it, Ken. Use your pig-headed brain. Would her family ever allow you to be married? She's practically a Duchess," Cynthia stood up and gave Kenneth's arm a squeeze. "And Duchesses marry Kings."

Kenneth felt something in himself deflating. Cynthia patted his arm and then she sighed, her eyes taking in the miserable expression on his face. "I'm sorry," she said, and she sounded as though she truly meant it. "But I beg you, brother. Don't let your heart get wrapped up in this. You're setting yourself up for a fall. Tell her about this Dillard character. Tell her that she needs to take precautions, then you leave it at that."

Kenneth had gone out late in the afternoon yesterday, and, not knowing where else to start, he'd visited the jailer. The man had told him that Jeb Dillard had never even arrived to see the constable. Confound it all. He should have known better than to entrust two of Dillard's working companions with the task.

Next, he visited the factory just beside the alley where Jeb had been employed, asking for Henry Berkshire, the foreman that had dismissed Jeb and given orders for him to be taken to the constable.

"Dillard, Dillard," said the man distractedly, ruffling a hand through his thinning black hair. "Jeb Dillard, you mean?"

"Yes, that's him."

"Right, the one who had a..." he hesitated, now tugging at his collar, "a disagreement, with the woman around the back there. Upsetting that was. I liked Jeb. He was a good worker."

"It's a shame he wasn't a better man," responded Kenneth, his jaw stiff.

"Yes, well, I hated to have to see him off," said Mr. Berkshire. It seemed, that to him, it didn't matter how despicable a man was if he happened to be a good worker. But perhaps Kenneth was reading too much in to the conversation.

"So, he hasn't been coming around here?"

"Jeb? I shouldn't think so. He should be awaiting a meeting with the courts. I spoke to the constable about the matter shortly after it happened."

"You did?"

"Yes," said the foreman, looking a little bewildered. "I thought the girl's father might be wanting to press charges."

"Dillard never arrived at the jailhouse," said Kenneth. He was eyeing Mr. Berkshire, trying to make out if he was telling him the truth.

The man touched the corner of his desk with the tips of his fingers. "Is that so?" he didn't seem as troubled as Kenneth might have hoped.

"Do you have the names of the men that were escorting him?"

"Err... no I don't. They weren't men from my crew."

Kenneth nodded, wracking his brains to try and remember their faces, but all that he could bring to mind was the furious, blood-splattered visage of Jeb Dillard. The memory made his blood boil.

There was a brief pause and then the foreman said: "Why all the questions, son?"

Kenneth disliked being called son; this man was only about five years his senior. He frowned. "I think Dillard might be hanging around. I'm afraid he might try something."

"Best let the authorities handle it," said Mr. Berkshire with a dismissive wave. "Don't want to be getting mixed up in anything unseemly."

"Do you mind if I have a word with a few members of your crew?" asked Kenneth. He'd just heard the echoing whistle that signaled the day's end.

"Help yourself," said the foreman, but he looked uneasy.

Kenneth had approached the gate as the workers were leaving. He edged his way through the crowd and came to a circle of five or six men that were packing their things away and chatting in heavy accents. One of the men froze when he noticed Kenneth approaching and nudged his companion.

"Excuse me," Kenneth said as he approached. "Could I have a word?"

Six pairs of eyes turned to Kenneth, all of them looking irritated that he was delaying them from leaving work for the day. But the two in the back of the group, he noticed, looked a little wary.

"I understand you men worked alongside Jeb Dillard."

One of the men grimaced and spat out a mouthful of tobacco. "We knew Jeb," he said. "What of him?"

"Can you tell me a bit about him?" he asked. "What was he like to work with?"

"Good man," said one of the six.

"Big mouth," said another.

The man who had spat looked Kenneth up and down. "You own the bakery over on 6th, right?"

"Yes, I do," said Kenneth, a little unnerved that he was so easily recognized.

"Yeah, well, I wouldn't want to mess around with Jeb Dillard," he advised. "Nasty temper, that one."

A man behind him protested. "He wasn't all bad," he said.

"Just 'cause you were in love with him don't mean we all were, Pruette," someone cracked.

"I'm just sayin'," said the man called Pruette. "I knew Jeb. We were on the boat together. He had a temper on him, but I never thought he was a..."

"I pulled him off a girl in the back alley a few weeks back," barked Kenneth.

Pruette shrugged. "Yeah, well, he was just having a bit of fun," muttered the man, but he took a step back as he caught the murderous look on Kenneth's face.

"Sounds like Jeb to me," said the first man that had spoken. "If we see him hanging about, we'll point ye in his direction."

"Much obliged," said Kenneth.

He could feel six pairs of eyes boring holes in his back as he turned and walked away.

Noelle was fanning the three cakes with vigor, an oven mitt in her hand as she knelt on the barstool.

"They look good, hmm?" she said to Kenneth, beaming.

They did. "We'll have to give them a bit to cool before we shape them," he said.

"Yes, yes," she appeared delighted with herself.

"Are you going to tell us what you did to the recipe?" asked Cynthia. "Why are they different colors?"

"So," said Noelle. "They're three different flavors of chocolate that I think will complement one another very nicely. This darker one is raspberry. The lightest is sort of a creamy, vanilla chocolate, and I'm not telling you what the middle one is."

"You're not telling," scoffed Cynthia. "How old are we now?"

Noelle merely winked, then she turned back to Kenneth. "How long do you think we should let them cool?"

Three hours and a lot of icing later, a marvelous confection of decorative rosebuds and plaintive, frosted peonies decorated the surface of Noelle's cake.

"It's perfect," said Noelle as she circled around the cutting table. "She'll love it."

Kenneth was sitting on the barstool, smiling in satisfaction as he popped another small bite of cake into his mouth from the pile of scraps still left on the table.

"What is it?" he demanded of Noelle, chewing slowly. "I can't figure out what you've done. It tastes better, different than my cake. Why?"

"Perhaps it is simply the hands that made it," suggested Noelle, mildly.

"You've put something in it," he insisted, taking another scrap.

Noelle was dusting off her hands on her apron. "I told you, I'm not telling."

"Crushed raspberries in the lower layer. Whipped egg whites, vanilla bean and powdered sugar for the top level..." he trailed off, still chewing. "What have you done with this one?"

Noelle giggled but instead of answering, she said: "Are you ready for tomorrow?"

Kenneth frowned. As excited as he was to see her again the following day, he wasn't entirely convinced he could portray the architect Noelle was hoping that he could for an entire weekend.

"I'm..."

"Please don't tell me you're having second thoughts," sighed Noelle. Her expression was dejected. As though the mere thought of his backing out of their plan had stolen all the happiness from her day.

"It's just..." he shrugged. "Noelle, I'm not an architect. How am I supposed to act the part?"

"Oh, it'll be easy. If someone asks, just come off all artsy and incredibly dull. Talk about the *feeling* or the *balance* of this structure or that. Once their eyes glaze over, they've stopped listening.

"What if we're found out?"

"Why should we be?"

Kenneth sighed, running his hand through his hair.

Noelle wandered around the table towards him. "Is it really going to be so dreadful?" she asked. "It's just a little party. But honestly, Mr. Black. I can cancel if you really don't want to come."

"Of course he wants to come!" Cynthia's shout from the front room destroyed the illusion of privacy Kenneth had been enjoying.

He sighed again. "I'll be there," he said, and then he flinched as Noelle clapped her hands loudly.

"Hooray!" she exclaimed. "I've been dreading this party for weeks. With you there…" her eyes lit upon his with a sweet intensity. "I can't imagine not enjoying myself."

Chapter Eight

Noelle was in a state of high anticipation. Guests were beginning to trickle into the house from every quarter. There were a handful of noblemen from London that her mother or aunt had some obscure connection to, their wives all seeming to possess thin, pinched faces like aunt Meldrid's. There were wealthy businessmen from here and there across the county, who all greeted her father as though they were the very best of long-standing friends, wringing his fingers and holding eye contact with him for a little too long. The contrast in the old money of London society and new wealth from New York and the surrounding areas was almost laughable.

Her father's friends all seemed to wear flamboyantly cut suits, their pocket watches gleaming on their waistcoats as though publicly declaring their wealthy status. Her mother's friends, however, were more inconspicuous. Each of the ladies that hung on her mother's arm seemed to possess the distinct sense of grace and poise that could only come from being high born. Their dresses were long and elegant and devoid of the sequins and glittering metallic taffeta that decorated the hemlines of many others, but Noelle knew, by the lines and cuts, that they could have easily fed an entire underclass family for a year.

These were things that normally didn't trouble her. Noelle stood apart from her parents, observing the comings and goings, and pondered the change in her line of thinking. She did used to enjoy these little get-togethers, when she was young. House parties were her very favorite, because it meant that there would be a whole host of other children to play with for an entire weekend. As she'd grown, however, the parties had become more and more wearisome. She'd tired of the endless, meaningless chatter and the many jibes about her age. She'd tired of the way the pimply sons of visiting wealth expected her to fall at their feet because they'd let their annual income slip in a casual conversation. And she'd missed her sisters something dreadful.

No, at that very moment, Noelle would have rather been climbing trees in the back garden than standing here feigning smiles at a variety of snobbish individuals who looked down their long noses at her and tried to find issue in the way she breathed.

But tonight would be different. Tonight... Noelle couldn't explain her feelings, but she felt that tonight was the start of something grand.

At that moment, Noelle spotted a familiar dirty-blonde head bobbling through the small crowd.

"Sarah!!!" she exclaimed, and she threw up her arms. Sarah-Jane's embrace was like balm. It calmed her and warmed a slight chill that had been creeping into her thoughts.

"How are you?" asked her elder sister. She peered concernedly into Noelle's face and Noelle felt as though she were being examined by a medical professional.

"I'm fine," said Noelle, and she nodded. "I've missed you. How was Italy?"

"Dreadfully far away from home," said Sarah-Jane, sighing. "It was lovely though."

"Where's Carson?" Fredrick Carson Williamson was Sarah-Jane's husband of three years. He was a handsome man with a light of adventure in his eyes. Sometimes, Noelle wondered how he had ended up falling for her sister, who was about as adventurous as an apple in an apple orchard. And yet they traveled extensively, allowing Carson to forge useful business connections for their father's company, as well as his own hotel on the New York coastline. The area drew a massive crowd each year, brought in by the horse races that took place on Brighton Beach. There was tell that one of the regular jockeys that rode at the Brighton Beach racecourse was actually a woman in disguise, but Noelle never put stock in any such nonsense.

"Oh, he's engrossed in some business talk or another already, I'm sure."

Noelle examined her sister just as critically as she had just examined her. "You look a bit peaky," she said. "Are you feeling alright? Did Italy disagree with you?"

"I'm just exhausted. We only got back last week. Thomas thought it was great fun. I thought we were going to have to leave him with a family of locals," she joked. "He told me he didn't like the big boat."

Noelle spotted her nephew then, weaving around the feet of the adults and smiling jovially.

"Auntie Nell, cookie?" he asked through a very toothy grin.

"Oh, Thomas, give your auntie a kiss," said Sarah-Jane. "She hasn't seen you in months!"

Noelle beamed down at him and stooped to scoop Thomas into her arms. "Very well," she whispered to him. "Let's see if we can't find you a cookie."

She began to make her way toward the kitchen with Thomas on her hip but was waylaid as Aunt Meldrid, her gown exquisitely pressed, cut across her path.

"Sarah-Jane! I had no idea you were coming," she said, stopping in front of Sarah and blocking Noelle's way forward.

"Oh, don't be silly Aunt Meldrid, you helped mother arrange the seating," said Noelle, rolling her eyes to the heavens.

"Well, how are we ever supposed to know where she is going to be?" said Aunt Meldrid, bending to bump her boney cheek against Sarah-Jane's in an imitation of a kiss. "She and that husband of hers are always scampering about jungles and mountains. Next she'll be living with the heretics in Greece."

"Aunt Meldrid!" Sarah-Jane reprimanded sharply. "I'll hear no more of that talk if you please, thank you very much."

"Oh, I say," their aunt ignored Sarah-Jane. "Have you seen the state of Cornella Forth's dress? Good heavens. You think they've fallen on hard times?"

"I have no idea, Auntie," said Sarah. She turned to Noelle. "Charlotte's train gets in tomorrow at ten, correct?"

Noelle nodded curtly.

"Why on Earth does she have to arrive a day later than everyone else?" complained Aunt Meldrid. "Were there no trains arriving earlier?"

"I should think it was something to do with Logan's company," said Noelle. "Really, shouldn't we be happy she's coming at all? They do live off in the Dakota Territory, after all."

"Yes, well, thank heavens she is coming. I don't think your poor mother could stand it if you girls weren't here. She's hurting more than she lets on, you know. Imagine a mother not knowing where her eldest daughter is. I'd hunt her down myself."

Their aunt was speaking of Dianna.

Thomas tugged on her collar. "Cookie? Auntie? Pwease?"

Not sorry for a reason to excuse herself, Noelle side-stepped her aunt and carried her nephew into the kitchen.

The room was in a flurry of chaos. Marcia was darting all around, shouting instructions at housemaids and helpers as she went. Noelle beamed at her as she entered.

"Thank goodness. Someone competent," grouched the cook. "Miss Noelle, please. I know you're busy, but will you please be a doll and whisk up a quick white sauce for me? We need a small vat of it, as apparently, we're feeding an army."

Noelle chuckled. "Just a moment," she said

She located the shortbread cookies in a jar over the counter and set two onto a tiny plate for Thomas.

"Here you go, love," she said to him as she sat him down on a chair next to the cutting table. "Auntie will be right back."

Pulling on an apron, Noelle set about helping her mentor with the massive dinner preparations. There were many grateful smiles sent in her direction. The household staff were accustomed to having Noelle pop in and out.

"I've got to run," she said to Marcia a half an hour later. "I'll be missed." Thomas was now happily munching on a third cookie. "Your momma's going to slaughter me," she said. "I'm sure your supper is ruined."

Thomas gave a happy belch in response, and Noelle, grinning, kissed him on the top of the head as she carried him back into the parlor room.

Noelle glanced around the room as she entered and passed Thomas off to his mother, who swiped at the crumbs on his tunic with a scowl.

"You completely abandoned me back there," she growled.

"Oh, my dear sister," laughed Noelle, "Aunt Meldrid is living in the house right now. I think I've done more than my fair share of covering Dianna's odd absences."

Sarah shook her head with a thin-lipped smile that did not entirely hide the pain behind her eyes.

"I miss her too," whispered Noelle, reaching out and grasping her sister's shoulder.

"I had another letter from her while we were away in Spain, I found it while I was going through the mail this morning. She enclosed a little photograph of her and her new family. She begged me to show you all."

"Where is it?!" Noelle squeaked. "Do you have it with you?"

"Not at the moment. We can run upstairs after dinner and have a look."

Noelle nodded excitedly.

Sarah-Jane offered Noelle a sad smile and then turned to look down at Thomas. "Did auntie give you a cookie?" she asked.

Thomas, grinning, held up three fingers, and Noelle slid away to the sideboard to pour herself a drink of water.

A shift in the air around her alerted her to his presence. He was a sudden warmth at her back and the room seemed to have become temporarily frozen.

"You look lovely."

Three words and Noelle could no longer breathe.

She smiled as Kenneth Black circled around to face her, his smile genuine and wonderfully kind.

"You came," she sighed, her eyes darting around his handsome features.

"I said I would."

He looked odd. Noelle was used to seeing Kenneth in plainclothes, an apron tied at his waist and flour smudged over his cheeks. This was something else altogether. He'd donned an impeccably cut suit in navy blue. His collar was starched high on his neck, and even as she watched, he gave it a little tug.

"You look smart," she said admiringly, her eyes scanning him of their own accord. His face was a bit red. "Is your tie too tight?"

"Actually, yes," said Kenneth, his ears going pink too. "Cynthia tied it and refused to loosen it. Now I can't get the blasted thing undone."

Noelle nodded covertly to a nearby alcove and together, they side-stepped behind the curtain.

"Let me see it," said Noelle, brushing Kenneth's hands aside and trying to ignore the charge that seemed to pulse through her fingertips as she touched him. "Look, see? There's a pin in it," she said matter-of-factly. She withdrew the pin and let out the knot a bit.

Kenneth let out a great gust of air that whooshed over her face and Noelle laughed. "Sorry," he said, "and thank you." He rubbed his neck, looking her over. "It's hot in here," he said at last.

"It'll be cooler when we head to the dining room, Mother's had the servants open the windows to the veranda."

"She couldn't open them herself?" Noelle stared at him. "Err. I meant. Sorry."

"Mr. Black..." Noelle started, a little offended by his callousness.

"Look," he interrupted. "I'm sorry. I'm hot and uncomfortable. I don't know any of these people, and I've yet to understand why on Earth you even want me here. I don't belong here, Miss Brittler."

"I..." she hesitated. "I told you that you didn't have to come."

"I know you did," said Kenneth. He glanced back over her shoulder and drew her further into the shadows. "But you asked me to do this for you," he whispered. "Here I am... but..."

"Noelle, darling, there you are!" Noelle jumped as her mother's voice rang out behind them like a bell. "Quit skulking in the corner, I need you to meet—," she broke off as she realized that Noelle wasn't alone. "Ahh, I don't believe that I have met your charming friend."

Noelle sat stunned for a moment. She'd been taken off-guard, and as such, every line she had practiced, every story she had come up with, they all fled her mind. She gawked at her mother, whose thin eyebrows began creeping steadily up her forehead and into her hairline.

"Mrs. Brittler," said Kenneth, he slid forward and bowed over her mother's hand. "It is an honor to meet you. Your daughter mentioned that you were turning twenty-five this year. A very happy birthday to you, Madame."

Samantha's suspicion appeared to drop like a stone into mud. "Twenty-five," she giggled. "Oh, indeed."

"Kenneth Black...more, at your service," Kenneth hesitated for a fraction of a second before adding to his last name, then he swept Noelle's mother a deep bow and said, "We were just admiring the framework of your lovely home." He indicated the window frame.

"Oh yes, Noelle did mention that you've a fondness for architecture Mr. Blackmore."

"Fondness!" Kenneth exclaimed, so loudly that both Noelle and her mother jumped. "My dear woman. I revere the structural soundness of a unique architectural design."

"Oh," Samantha chuckled, looking at Noelle, who was having a difficult time hiding her smile. "My apologies."

"Not at all. Not at all, dear lady! Come," Kenneth extended his arm to her, taking hold of her hand and tucking it into his elbow without asking. Then, with his head held high, he strode forward. "Let us examine the ceilings of your home. I would love to know the designer. Such a fantastic infrastructure."

Noelle couldn't help it. She ducked behind the curtain and laughed silently into her hand.

"Noelle?" she could hear her mother's desperate voice calling her as Kenneth led her on into her own parlor. "Aren't you coming?"

"Yes!" Noelle squeaked, and she hurried to catch up with them.

Kenneth was still expounding on the glories of the house's structure when Noelle joined them. Her mother raised her eyebrows at her. The expression said, quite clearly, 'This is the wealthy architect you took a fancy to in the market?' Noelle could tell that Kenneth was successfully boring her mother to death, and she smiled indulgently as she turned to listen to Kenneth ramble.

"If you'll excuse me, Mr. Blackmore, I believe I have just spotted a new arrival across the way," said her mother, and in a moment, she had flitted between two guffawing gentlemen and vanished.

"You could take it down a notch if you wanted," said Noelle, taking Kenneth's arm and giggling behind her hand.

"What?" asked Kenneth, his grin widening. "I thought I did rather well."

Noelle rolled her eyes at him.

A gong sounded from downstairs and Kenneth looked around, evidently confused. "What was that?"

Noelle giggled again. "It's the dinner gong," she said. In twos and threes, the small crowd of close friends and influential guests made their way through the door at the opposite end of the room and into the dining hall. Noelle saw Kenneth's eyes widen as they entered together and he gave a low whistle.

"You know I've never set foot in a place like this before," he said under his breath. "Never imagined I would ever have a reason to unless I was bringing in the cake."

"I think your sister already took care of that for us," said Noelle and she indicated the massive confection of sugared cream and roses displayed immaculately on the sideboard just behind the head of the table. "We did well, didn't we? I'm rather proud of myself."

"You should be," said Kenneth. He gave her hand a small pat where it rested in the crook of his elbow and Noelle felt her stomach swoop as though she had just dived off Fenton's Pier.

She swallowed past the sudden dryness in her throat and led Kenneth toward the middle of the table, where they had seats side by side. "I told mother I was intrigued with you so that she would seat us side by side."

"And was that a lie?"

Noelle looked at him. Kenneth was smiling, but his eyes were curious. She could tell he genuinely wanted to know the answer.

"Certainly not. I find you very intriguing Mr. Black...more."

"Good," he said, and then, acting every inch the gentleman, he strode forward to pull out the seat that carried her name card.

"Thank you, sir," she said mildly, and she pulled her skirts to the side so that she could navigate the narrow space.

Champagne sat in fluted glasses all along the table, and Noelle and Kenneth were afforded a bit of privacy by an enormous flower arrangement dominating the center of the scene. No expense had been spared. The silver was all freshly polished and the china plates shone in the candlelight from a massive chandelier dangling overhead.

As Noelle glanced around, she suddenly felt embarrassed. These things. The shining, ostentatious display. It was all a bit garish. How had she never noticed before? She'd always known her mother's tastes ran toward the dramatic, but this was... She glanced sideways at Kenneth. Darling, sweet Kenneth, who'd lost so much, who'd built his small business from nothing. What would he think of her after tonight? Would he even want to stay?

Her father stood up at the head of the table and the polite chatter around the room faded. "Thank you all for coming," he said. "I must say, I'm very pleased to see you all here to celebrate the best thing that ever happened to me." He extended a hand to his wife and Samantha stood up beside him, her cheeks pink with embarrassment. A few of the onlookers chuckled. "My beautiful wife, ladies and gentlemen. Samantha Brittler. Happy Birthday, darling." And beneath many scandalized gazes, he kissed her.

Noelle shook her head. She liked to think of her father as reasonable and level-headed. He loathed dramatic scenes and scandal as much as her mother, unless of course, he was the one causing the scandal. As one of the most powerful men in the state of New York, if Thomas Brittler wanted to kiss his wife, he would do it whenever and however he liked.

A few members of the party cleared their throats uncomfortably. Then somebody wolf-whistled. Her parents broke apart and Noelle chuckled, wondering how many glasses of wine her father had had before his little speech. "To my wife!!!" he shouted, raising his glass.

The cry was echoed all around. "To Mrs. Brittler!!" Samantha blushed as the room drank to her.

"Now," said her father. "I trust your rooms are all comfortable?"

There was a murmur of agreement.

"Good, good. After dinner and cake, the men are invited to join me in the gaming room," he finished. "I wish you all a fabulous weekend stay at the Brittler Family Estate." The room rang with the sound of a polite round of applause, and Noelle watched her father resume his seat and lean towards his—still scarlet—wife.

"I like your father," said Kenneth quietly.

Noelle turned to look at him. He was grinning at her. "Yes, he's quite the character," she said.

She leaned back as a footman placed a steaming salmon filet on the table before her. "Thank you," she whispered to him. His name was Johnathon, and he was new to the Brittler household. "Tell Marcia I said it looks fabulous. She's outdone herself."

The footman nodded and gave her a small smile as he moved to place the next plate beside Kenneth, who thanked him also. He was one of the few who did. Why had Noelle never noticed this before? Many of the guests acted as though the servants were invisible as their dinner magically appeared in front of them.

She noticed their butler, Hendrix, giving Johnathon the eye. Hendrix ran the household. He was a firm, upright sort of man, hired by her mother when she had first moved to America and married her father. As far as Noelle knew there were only three households in New York that hired as many hands as the Brittler Family Estate and from what her mother said, it wasn't nearly enough. Apparently, things were done very differently in England, but father had insisted that a butler, a cook, two handmaids, two footmen and a few men to do odd jobs around the estate were more than enough. Noelle privately agreed.

Her father had purchased the house and its surrounding acreage in 1856, just before her eldest sister Dianna was born. It was vast, and castle-like, with three floors and even a small turret in the upstairs library. Noelle had always loved growing up here, but once her sisters had left, the house had felt a bit forlorn. Little by little, the city of Manhattan crept closer to them, until the Brittler Family Estate was one of the largest remaining holdings on the island. Her father refused to give an inch of land for development. Not to factories or cottages, not for the right price, not at all. It was very like him to claim something as his own. Once he did, he never seemed to let it go.

"So," whispered Kenneth in her ear, bringing her out of her contemplation. "After cake, I'll join the rest of the men?"

"Naturally," said Noelle, smiling indulgently.

"I'm not so sure about that," he said, frowning as he cut into his meal. "I don't know any of these men."

"I'll introduce you to my father," she said.

But Kenneth continued to frown all the way through dinner. Noelle wondered what was on his mind. Was he truly so uncomfortable in her surroundings? If so, she thought this was a bit unfair. She'd adapted well enough to his home, why couldn't he make the same effort for her?

"What is it?" she asked him quietly.

"Not now," he said.

Noelle fidgeted. Her hands twisting the corner of her napkin in her lap. Had she made a terrible mistake? Kenneth must have noticed her distress, because his warm palm came down gently on top of her fingers.

"Later," he whispered, and he gave her a gentle smile.

Noelle felt her shoulders relax, and she spent the rest of the meal conversing idly with the woman next to her.

She was a round figure, with a second chin wobbling beneath her first as she ate.

"Amelia Gene Stovich," she proclaimed herself, "Wife of Reginald Stovich, the noted spice merchant. And you are the charmingly single daughter, are you not?"

Noelle swallowed her forkful of salmon rather harder than she had meant to and hastily reached for her glass.

"That would be me," she said through a cough.

"It was meant to be a joke," said Amelia Stovich, slapping Noelle on the back with such vigor, she nearly knocked her into the table. "I suppose you tire of having your marital status dissected by a bunch of doddery old fools though, don't you?"

Noelle stared at her for a moment and then she laughed. "Yes, it does get rather exhausting at times." She took another drink of water and cleared her throat quietly into her hand.

"Yes," said Amelia. "Well, my dear, if you don't want to marry, then don't. That's my advice."

This time, Noelle managed to stop herself from choking, but it was a near miss. Never in her life had someone portrayed the single life of a spinster as a viable option. Never, and yet this woman mentioned it in passing, as if it were a throw-away suggestion of no real importance.

"You wait," she continued. "You wait until you find that one man. The good one. You know what I mean," She elbowed Noelle in the ribs. "The one that *means* something, dear. The one that changes the way you look at things without even meaning to. Don't listen to any of these other namby-pamby, ritzy folk. You do what makes you happy. And you know what?" Amelia Gene Stovich fixed Noelle with a hard stare. "If you don't find that special one, it's not all that bad."

Noelle shook her head incredulously, a massive grin spreading over her cheeks, and then she raised her glass to Amelia. "To a life not all that bad," she said, and then she drank. Amelia laughed, her second chin trembling hither and thither.

"To a life not all that bad," she echoed and she drank too.

Amelia Gene Stovich was clearly an American woman that had married one of Noelle's father's associates. She couldn't be one of her mother's friends from England, she was much too forward, and her wealth was evident in the ruby-studded necklace Noelle could see just poking from beneath her large neck.

"That's pretty," said Noelle, indicating the gemstones.

"Reginald gave it to me on our first anniversary," said Amelia proudly. She thrusted her ample chest forward to better display the jewels.

"Have you been married long?" Noelle asked.

"Twenty-two years next March. That's him over there," she said, indicating a little bean-pole of a man across the table who was staring at her with something akin to adoration on his face. Amelia twiddled her fingers at him, and then giggled like a school-girl when he gave her a roguish wink.

Noelle felt a spike of envy rise in her chest. The couple's happiness reminded her of her parents. Something she'd always strove for. "How did you meet?"

"Honestly?" Amelia looked down at Noelle, who was several inches shorter than her. "He came to Michigan to cultivate a plantation. I was a shop girl in a small town there and something just," she snapped her thick fingers over her dinner plate.

"That is lovely," said Noelle.

"Isn't it?" Amelia Stovich beamed at her. "Wait for the right one, my dear, and when he comes along, don't you let him go." She winked.

Just then, Noelle's father stood once more at the head of the table. The servants were quickly and silently clearing away the third course. "If I'm not much mistaken," said Thomas Brittler, "I believe it is the perfect time for a small chorus of Happy Birthday!"

Behind him, a footman was touching a match to a handful of candles that had been set at intervals over the top of the cake. Kenneth caught her eye, and his smile spoke volumes. Noelle's chest swelled as the cake was sat down in front of her mother, who beamed around as the whole room chorused: "Happy Birthday tooooo yooou-uu."

Next to her, Amelia Stovich bellowed loudest of all, and Noelle couldn't stop grinning.

CHAPTER NINE

"SHOW ME! SHOW ME!" Thomas was dancing beside the bed Sarah-Jane would share with him and her husband for the next few nights.

Noelle squeezed her eyes shut tight, fighting away the tears that had sprung up there.

"Be quiet, Thomas," said Sarah. She sat down beside Noelle and put her arm around her.

"She's glorious," said Noelle, running her fingers over the photograph. "She has father's nose, look!"

"I know," said Sarah-Jane, smiling.

"He's rather terrifying though, isn't he?" said Noelle, indicating the stone-faced Native-American man who stood beside Dianna, his hand possessive on her slender shoulder.

"He is a bit," agreed Sarah, shifting slightly to peer over Noelle's arm. "He's huge."

Thomas was becoming more agitated the longer he was ignored. "Pwease?" he begged again, but very quietly. Noelle smiled and reached for him.

Her nephew tucked himself into her arms and grinned as she handed him the photograph. "Be careful not to rip it," instructed his mother, and Thomas nodded as he took the picture from Noelle.

"Can I read her letter?" Noelle asked.

Sarah unfolded the bit of parchment in her hand and passed it to Noelle, who took it as she swiped away the tears in her eyes.

My Dearest Sarah-Jane,

Thank you for your last letter. I loved the photographs. I've enclosed one of my own. We hadn't had any at all because Shiye said that the camera made him nervous, but I managed to talk him into it after he'd seen yours.

I can't believe how fast our children are growing. Thomas looked so big sitting on your lap. He looks a lot like his father.

Things have been quiet here. Rose has begun to crawl. She scoots herself over the floor and gets mad when we pick her up. She's very independent.

Noelle could hear the humor in her sister's words and she ached to see her niece scooting her way over the floor. More tears fell.

Show everyone the photo, won't you? I'm afraid we could only afford the one.

I sent mother a gift as well. Tell her happy birthday for me. It breaks my heart that we can't come home to celebrate with her, but I doubt she would want us there anyhow.

"I hate that she thinks that," said Noelle. She reached into her sleeve and withdrew a handkerchief.

"Mother hasn't exactly been kind to her since she left," said Sarah-Jane, dabbing at her own eyes.

"I realize," muttered Noelle. "But she's been different lately. It's like she's trying desperately to cling to her old ways, but it just isn't working. Can you imagine what she would have done five years ago if Father had tried to kiss her in front of a whole crowd of people like that?"

Sarah-Jane laughed out loud at this.

"She can't come home anyhow, remember? They're in hiding, and imagine how Mother would behave if an Indian came walking in through the front parlor."

"This isn't the life I imagined for her," whispered Noelle.

"I doubt it's the life she imagined for herself," chuckled Sarah. "But you do have to admit, she seems very happy."

Noelle nodded and continued to read.

The river is just warm enough to swim in now. Shiye has built a dam upstream a ways so that we can have a swimming hole to cool off in in these summer months.

I want to hear all about your visit to Spain when you return.

Tell darling little Thomas that his auntie loves him and give my best to your husband.

Love Always,

Dianna

Noelle let her eyes return to the picture, which Thomas had discarded on the bedspread.

"I'm glad she sent this. I was wondering who Rose looked like."

"I have to remember to show Charlotte when she arrives tomorrow," said Sarah. "Now," she turned her entire body to face Noelle, who gulped. "Tell me about this architect from Ireland."

If it wouldn't have been a giveaway, Noelle would have flinched. Instead, she straightened her shoulders and met Sarah's curious gaze with one of defiance.

"What about him?" she asked testily.

"Well..." said Sarah, her voice heavy with suggestion. "No one seems to know who he is for a start. All that mother would tell me is that he's very accomplished in his field.

"He is."

"That you met him in the shops in town."

"I did."

"And that you've taken a fancy to him."

"I have."

"Have you, really?!" squawked Sarah-Jane excitedly.

Noelle, realizing too late what she had said, groaned. "Must you pry and poke?" she begged. "Can't you just let the matter rest? Nothing is going to come of it."

"Nothing!" laughed Sarah. "I saw the way you were looking at one another at dinner."

"Saaarah," moaned Noelle, burying her face in a throw pillow.

"So, what's he like?"

"He's..." Noelle paused, lifting her head off the bed and contemplating the far wall. "Different," she finished finally, and she buried her face once more.

"Oh, come off it," giggled Sarah-Jane, and she shoved at Noelle, forcing her to roll onto her side. "He's very handsome," she said.

"You keep your paws off, sister; you're already married to your own handsome man."

Sarah-Jane swelled importantly. "I know I am," she said. Thomas was watching his mother and aunt with wide eyes.

"I'm a handom man," he said, frowning.

Sarah broke down into peals of laughter and Noelle seized Thomas and tossed him over her head. He giggled as she caught him. "Yes, you are! The most handsome man I've ever met!"

"I beg your pardon," a voice in the doorway made the girls look up. Their father was standing there, grinning at the sight of his daughters and grandson playing. "You're being missed downstairs," he said with a wink.

"Oh, Father, look!" Noelle caught hold of the photograph of Dianna and her family and thrust it under his nose.

It seemed to take him a moment to realize what he was seeing, and then his eyes became rather misty.

"So that's them, is it?" he said with a small smile. "There's my son-in-law and my little granddaughter. Good heavens but she looks like him."

"Look at her nose though," said Sarah softly, coming right up to him and squeezing his arm. "It's just like yours."

"Her eyes look like her mom too," said Noelle, bending in for a closer inspection.

"Well," said Thomas, wiping at his eyes. "Isn't that something?" He smiled, and the girls hugged him.

Then he spotted Thomas on the floor. "There you are, little man!" he said jovially, bending to scoop him up. "Shall we head back down to the party then? I bet it's only an hour or two until your bedtime!" Thomas laughed as his grandfather tickled him, heading out of the room and down the hallway.

Noelle grinned at the sound and then, after a final glance at the photograph in her hand, she set it down on Sarah-Jane's nightstand and followed them out of the room.

Chapter Ten

Kenneth was completely out of his element. He stayed quiet in the corner, playing a few hands of cards and enjoying a few glasses of flavorful brandy that he certainly wouldn't have been able to afford at home. It was with relief that he greeted Thomas Brittler's suggestion that they rejoin the ladies for a nightcap.

When he entered the parlor room however, he couldn't spot Noelle anywhere, and she would be hard to miss. She was a vision tonight. Her hair was piled high on the top of her head, revealing her slender neck, which looked in need of more than a little kissing. Her dress was white and beige, form-fitting and low cut. He wondered if she could see his thoughts written on his face all evening.

The Brittlers' servants had placed him in a large room. Honestly, he had protested, supposing they had placed him in a room for visiting dignitaries and whatnot. But the servant had insisted that this was his room. It was fabulous. Twice the size of the tiny apartment above the bakery that Kenneth shared with his sister and five times as grand. The head and foot of the bed were made of intricately carved wood, and the coverlet was made of soft cotton.

He felt rather guilty as he poured himself another finger of brandy, staring idly around the room. Noelle's mother, Samantha Brittler, seemed to be enjoying herself. She was seated on a chaise lounge in the center of the room, surrounded by her friends, who were all gossiping happily.

Then at last, there she was, striding in through the open door that led to the foyer and the massive staircase that circled to the upper floors. Her skin seemed to shimmer in the candlelight, and she looked joyous, and yet somehow forlorn. Kenneth frowned as Noelle glanced around the room—for him, he assumed—but a moment later she had fallen into conversation with a young man who looked to be about the same age as her. Twenty-two or Twenty-three at least. The sight aged Kenneth in his own eyes somehow. He was nearing his thirtieth birthday, after all. Did Noelle see him as too old for her, perhaps?

An unbidden emotion rose up inside him just then, and he fought to suppress it. She was not his to claim, but oh, he wanted her. He wanted to claim her, to tell the world she was his. To demand that this handsome young suitor kept his hands off her. Kenneth's nostrils flared as the boy reached up to Noelle's face and twirled an errant curl around his finger. Noelle laughed and slapped his hand away, but the boy was smiling, and Kenneth was furious. He threw the last of his brandy into his mouth and set the glass down on a nearby table. It made a loud clunking sound, but Kenneth didn't hear it.

He smiled as he strode over to Noelle and her new friend. "I don't believe we've been introduced," he said, sticking out his hand and forcing the boy to take a step back.

"Uh, no, you're correct sir," he said.

"Kenneth Blackmore, sir," said Kenneth mockingly and he grasped the boy's hand tightly.

"Wallace Gerson," said the boy. He did not wince as Kenneth shook his entire body with a rather vigorous handshake. "Um... How do you know the Brittlers, Mr. Blackmore?"

"Oh, I don't actually," said Kenneth. "I'm just here for the free food," Wallace Gerson laughed, but Noelle did not. On the contrary, she frowned at him. He amended himself with a genial smile.

"Noelle and I met in town the other day and she did me the honor of inviting me to her mother's birthday celebrations. I'm told we're in for quite the weekend of festivities."

"So I hear, so I hear," chuckled Wallace. "I was just asking Miss Brittler if she would like to accompany me on an evening stroll... so if you will excuse—."

"Splendid idea, sir!" cried Kenneth. "Miss Noelle, would you like me to retrieve your wrap for you?"

"Um, no, Mr. Blackmore, thank you. It's a warm night, I think."

Wallace Gerson was looking uncomfortable. He was frowning at Kenneth, who stared back benignly, feigning a look of complete innocence. With a raised eyebrow at Noelle, he led the way to the foyer.

"Are you drunk, Mr. Blackmore?" Noelle hissed in his ear as they both followed Gerson's winding path through the crowded room.

"Drunk? Certainly not." He was far from drunk. He might be a bit hot around the collar, but it would take more than a few licks of brandy to make him unsteady on his feet.

"Then why are you behaving like a complete fool?" she hissed.

"Why?" ask Kenneth, grinning. "Have I interrupted something?"

Noelle glared at him, and then her eyes softened.

"No, not really," she said, sighing. "Wallace Gerson is an old family friend. We've known one another since we were small."

"Is that so. Has he always had a soft spot for you then?"

"Wallace? Not at all."

"Interesting..." said Kenneth. But there had been no mistaking the light of challenge that had flared in the boy's eyes when Kenneth had insisted on accompanying them. Kenneth had to remind himself that he wasn't a challenger, he wasn't anything, he wasn't even competition. Not when it came to Noelle. She wasn't anything to him... she *couldn't ever* be anything to him. And yet, she was.

The night was mild, as Noelle had said. She smiled as they strolled through the front door and wandered out into the back garden. The path alongside the house was lit dimly with the light from the windows.

"How have you been keeping?" asked Wallace. He was directing all his attention onto Noelle, and Kenneth could tell that the boy was trying to shut him out.

"Quite well, actually," responded Noelle, her smile easy and warm. She was obviously very comfortable with Mr. Wallace Gerson. The thought made Kenneth's jaw ache.

"Been missing your sisters, though, I'd imagine," said Gerson. "Where are they all now?" Off on various misadventures? Is Sarah-Jane home yet?"

"Sarah-Jane is actually here tonight with her husband and son," said Noelle happily. "Charlotte is arriving tomorrow morning."

"Oh, I didn't see Sarah in all the hubbub," said Gerson. "I'll have to be sure to say hello before the night is out. You know how she hates to be ignored." They both laughed.

The three of them were strolling along a garden path that was hardly wide enough for two people, forcing Kenneth to step behind the pair. If Gerson's goal was to shut him out, he was doing a very good job. He'd known Noelle had sisters, but he had never thought to ask their names. He knew very little about her life, and Gerson's intimate knowledge was putting him at a disadvantage.

"Was your sister traveling?" Kenneth asked Noelle, but it was Gerson who answered.

"In Spain," he said, turning his head half an inch towards Kenneth as he spoke. Noelle, however, turned completely around.

"Isn't that just marvelous?!" she said. "Spain. I hear it's absolutely beautiful."

"Ah yes," said Kenneth, "the architecture there is stunning."

"Have you been to Spain then?" asked Gerson, finally turning around to face him as well.

"Just the one time," said Kenneth quickly.

Noelle's eyebrows shot up.

"I was commissioned for a job there when I was first starting out. Unfortunately, I wasn't able to see much of the countryside, as I was assisting Antoni Gaudi with the construction of the Sagrada Familia."

Gerson's mouth dropped open in shock. Kenneth had to fight the urge to lift it with one finger and pop his mouth closed again. Just seeing the look on the boy's face made him wish that the lie he was telling was even somewhat true. Gravel was crunching noisily under their feet as they walked. He wondered if he dared glance at Noelle. He found that he did dare.

She was smirking at him and shaking her head, but she didn't look angry. He let out a breath he hadn't realized he'd been holding. Gerson was still looking at him. He had closed his mouth.

"So, you've lived in Barcelona?" he choked. He was quickly regaining his composure.

"Not for long," said Kenneth, "and when I was there..." he shook his head sadly, "Spain pains me," he added quietly. "Shall we change the subject. What is it you do for a living, Mr. Gerson?"

Wallace seemed to swallow painfully hard, because he winced, and then he relaxed into himself once more. "My father owns a string of profitable hotels in and out of the country. I assist in the management."

"Oh, I see, you're a hotel manager," said Kenneth. "Good for you." Gerson's responding smile was wooden, and Noelle appeared suddenly overtaken with a fit of coughing.

Kenneth was rigidly aware that, in the real world, this boy ranked far above him, but it was rather fun to watch him squirm.

"Shall we go in? It's a bit chilly, isn't it?" Gerson's next question was directed to Noelle once more.

Kenneth noticed the emphasis on the word 'we' and did not like it.

"I think I might stay outside for a bit longer, actually," said Kenneth, making a valiant effort to conceal the note of smugness in his voice. "Why don't you head on in."

"Noelle?" Gerson looked at her with quiet desperation.

"I think I'll stay outside a bit longer as well," she said.

If Kenneth had been a beast, he would have roared in victory.

With a stiff nod to both of them, Wallace Gerson marched back up the path without a backward glance.

"That was cruel," said Noelle, the moment he was out of earshot.

Kenneth looked around at her. "I don't know what you're talking about," he said, offering her his arm. She took it, and Kenneth began to hum tunelessly as they made their way further up the garden path.

"Where on Earth did you get that story? 'Spain pains me,'" she quoted at him, smirking all over her pretty face.

He smiled wickedly. "Did you like that bit?"

"Much the best way to insure Wallace did not question you any further," said Noelle.

"That's what I thought!" he declared. They turned around the corner of the house. "Your cake was astoundingly delicious, by the way."

Noelle's eyes lit with his complement. "Did you really think so?"

"I wasn't the only one who thought so. Didn't you hear Mrs. Amelia *Gene* Stovich? She was all but declaring ownership of every uneaten piece."

"You be nice, Kenneth. I liked her rather a lot."

He chuckled. "I did too. Straight forward. I like that in a woman."

Noelle threw back her head and laughed.

"You're in similar company," she said cheekily, peering up at him through her long eye lashes.

"I'm aware of it," muttered Kenneth. They were very close now. Kenneth could feel every indent the tips of her fingers were making in his arm as she clung to him.

Without really thinking about it, he led her deeper into the shadows. They were alone. Completely alone, for the very first time since they had met. Kenneth remembered her defiance that day, and her fury. And his own fury flared suddenly in his chest as he remembered Jeb Dillard and the threat he still posed. He would protect her from this. He would protect her from anything.

The night was as silent as it ever was in the city. Factories chugged in a melancholy way in the distance. Insects chirped all around them, and light sparkled in brief patches from the high windows of the Brittlers' home.

"I'm very glad you decided to come," whispered Noelle. Kenneth looked down at her and said, with more truth than he thought the words would've ever possessed:

"I am too."

"And thank you,"

"For what?" They were moving away from the lighted windows now, both of them smiling. With the threat of Wallace Gerson successfully vanquished, Kenneth was hovering in some brief happy place with Noelle by his side.

"For allowing me the use of your help and expertise in baking my mother's cake. For agreeing to come to the party at all..." she hesitated, her eyes on the gravel path in front of them. "For your kindness, and your uncanny ability to make me laugh..."

She smiled at him. Sweetly, coyly, and Kenneth wondered what she would say if she knew what he was thinking right now. The moonlight glittered off her face and hair. She looked so beautiful at that moment. Her cheeks were flushed with the pleasure of his company, and her lips... Kenneth wondered how they would look if he were to kiss her for hours. How pink could he make her cheeks? How warm would she feel against him? She was still looking up at him, waiting for his response.

Before he could stop himself, Kenneth had pulled them to a halt and taken her face in both his hands. Noelle froze, and he saw a curiosity in her eyes as they roved over his face.

"I don't think..." she whispered, covering his hands with her smaller, softer ones.

And then Kenneth kissed her. Before she could tell him they needed to stop. Before she could tell him that they could never be together. Tonight, he would be anything for her. Tonight, he wished he were.

She was soft, warm, and delicious, and to his delight, she yielded to him without a single protest. He angled her head up, taking full possession of her mouth. His lips moved over hers with a fervor that he couldn't begin to justify. He'd never kissed a woman like this before, not with this much abandon, this much need.

She broke the kiss, pulling away from him. "Kenneth, I..."

He tugged her lips back to his. Guiding her hands to his chest, begging her to give into him once more. He could feel the heat between them increasing; he could feel her melting into his embrace. She was perfect. She was the only thing he could feel, and he'd never felt anything properly before.

The sound of crunching gravel made them jerk apart. He released Noelle so suddenly that she lost balance. His hand on hers steadied her, and both of them, their faces flushed with the heat of their kisses, turned to greet the newcomer.

It was Gerson. Kenneth wanted to scoop up a handful of rocks from the path and chase the boy away like a stray dog. He couldn't stop himself glaring at him through the darkness. He glanced at Noelle. She was composed, if a little pinker than she had been a moment ago.

Kenneth wondered if Gerson knew what he had just interrupted.

"They're going up," he said, still standing three yards away from them. "I thought you ought to know."

"Thank you, Wallace, dear," Noelle called. She wouldn't meet Kenneth's eyes. "I suppose we'd better go in," she said to him.

He thought about reaching for her, stopping her as she moved swiftly away from him. He needed to know what she was thinking, but he couldn't say anything to her in front of Gerson.

With a grumble and a sigh, he tailed after her into the house.

CHAPTER ELEVEN

NOELLE THANKED THE LORD for the darkness outside, and for the fact that many of the candles had already been doused by the servants by the time she set foot in the foyer. Her cheeks were on fire. She could feel her heart racing in her chest.

Above her, she could make out the sounds of their many guests heading to their appointed bedchambers for the night.

She caught sight of a barrel-chested figure in the doorway, and for a moment, she froze, terrified, recalling Jeb and his threat.

"What is it?!" Kenneth had come into the hall just behind her. "Who's there?"

By the time Kenneth had reached her, Noelle's breath had returned to her.

"Hendrix," she whispered on a sigh of relief.

The family butler grinned at her. "Did you have a pleasant stroll?" he asked nonchalantly. His eyes flickered toward Kenneth and back again.

"It was rather enjoyable," responded Kenneth without missing a beat. Noelle frowned over her shoulder at the smugness in his voice.

Hendrix's sharp eyes slid over Kenneth, and Noelle had the distinct impression he was sizing him up. His look was calculating and Kenneth shifted from foot to foot as the silence between the three of them lengthened.

Wallace sidled through the still-open door.

"Heading up, Mr. Gerson?" Hendrix was all form again, his voice unctuous. "Shall I put your coat away with the rest?"

Gerson shrugged out of his jacket without looking at any of them. "Thank you, Hendrix."

He passed Noelle on his way upstairs, his face turned away from her. Frowning, she caught his sleeve. "Aren't you going to wish me a goodnight?" she asked. Wallace spun back to her, and Noelle saw that his face was chalky-white. "My dear Wallace, are you well?"

He blinked at her, and then some color made its way into his cheeks. He bent at the knee, bowing his head over her hand and pressed a lingering kiss to her knuckles.

"My lady," he said formally against her fingers, and Noelle felt a strange shiver run down her spine. "Sweet dreams," he whispered. And without another word or a backward glance, Wallace darted up the stairs and turned the corner, heading for his bedroom in the west wing of the house.

Noelle made her way up more slowly, frowning at the back of her friend's head in confusion. Wallace had never in his life looked at her like that before.

"You speak to me of cruelty," muttered a voice in her ear.

Noelle looked around at Kenneth, flummoxed. "What do you mean?"

"How long have you been leading him to believe something was growing between the two of you?"

Noelle froze, her foot hovering a few inches above the top stair, and turned to look at Kenneth, whose smile was a little forced.

"I never... he doesn't think—."

"My dear," said Kenneth gently, sidling past her and turning to face her with a look that spoke volumes. "That boy is head over heels in love with you."

Noelle's foot landed on the top step with a thud. "Don't be so ridiculous," she told Kenneth, incredulous.

"Wallace and I have been friends for years. Since we were children, really."

Kenneth nodded. "That does make sense," he said. He bent and took hold of her hand, just as her childhood friend had a few moments ago. His eyes never left hers as he bent and brushed his lips over her knuckles. Noelle felt the place where his mouth had touched her burn.

"I'll see you in the morning," he whispered, and then he dropped her hand and strode away from her, leaving Noelle feeling bereft. She willed him to look back and offer her a smile. Willed him to ease the uncomfortable ache that had blossomed in her chest at his words. But Kenneth did not look back, and as Noelle turned and made her way down the darkened corridor to her room, she could still hear his words echoing in her ears.

"That boy is head over heels in love with you."

She didn't sleep. Noelle lay awake late into the night. Her heart felt as though it had vacated her chest. Where it had beat— where it had *pounded*— just hours ago, was a concave hole. She imagined the look on Wallace's face as he kissed her goodnight. There was no mistaking the hurt in his eyes. Had she done that to him?

She thought of Wallace as a boy. He had played with her when she was a child. Much closer to her age than that of any of her elder sisters, they had galloped around the garden on toy horses while her sisters sat at picnics. She had grown beside him, always admiring his kindness, and his freckles, which were like hers, spattered across his nose. His eyes always crinkled when he smiled at her.

He had always teased her about her suitors, saying this one was paunchy or that one was much too old for her. If he had had any interest in being with her, why had he never said as much. *Perhaps he has,* said a small voice in the back of her mind.

Noelle sifted through her memories. When they were eight, Wallace had kissed her behind a large curtain hanging from an upstairs window during a game of hide and seek. "Don't tell!" he had said immediately, and Noelle grinned as she remembered the boyish panic in his gaze. She had teased him about it for years now, never thinking anything of it. Perhaps her teasing had cost him his nerve?

She stared at the swooping pink canopy above her head. Wallace was very handsome. His hair was brown and his pale face was dotted with freckles, just as hers was. He was lean, but not too skinny, with a smile that could frighten away the rain clouds on even the cloudiest of days. He had always been her Wallace. Dear, dear Wallace. Her playmate and her friend.

She wondered if she had missed some sort of sign, or perhaps led him on without meaning to. *I'd have known, wouldn't I?* Wouldn't she have known if her closest friend had been trying to become closer to her all along?

Her mind turned to Kenneth. He was masculine and warm and completely off limits. Why had she brought him here? What good could possibly have come from forcing him to remain in her presence? But... she hadn't wanted to let him go. Not yet. Deep in her absent heart, Noelle knew that she was only prolonging the inevitable. Kenneth, despite her completely outrageous attraction to him, was never a possibility. Never and that was that. Noelle shoved the idea away from her, afraid that if she paused too long to consider the matter, she would attempt to change her own mind.

And what of that kiss? Noelle lifted her fingers to her mouth and traced the place where Kenneth's lips had captured her own. She had never been kissed. It wasn't that she had never been kissed like that... Noelle had never been kissed at all. Not since she was eight years old and ensconced in folds and folds of dusty window hangings. Not since she had become a woman.

Kenneth had tasted of need. He had been possessive and powerful and all-consuming. Noelle had never imagined that one kiss could turn her life so utterly upside down. She thought of the way he had held her. Desperately, as if he understood that their time together was short and he was determined to make her feel some part of this need he had before he was forced to let her go.

But would she ever find the strength to let *him* go? After he had stolen her breath and crept into the very depths of her mind, would she be able to say goodbye? What was to stop her from visiting the bakery every day once this was over? What was to stop her from...

Noelle thought of Dianna. Gone. So far away from them all. Married to a man so far beneath her that their mother couldn't bear to think of her. She couldn't do that to her family.

In her younger years, Noelle had told herself that if she ever found love, she would cling to it with both hands. She had leapt at the chance of meeting new suitors; she had thrown her emotions at their feet and encouraged her sisters to do the same. But her feelings had been trodden on a few times too many. The man that she had always dreamed of sharing her life with... she had begun to lose faith in the idea of his very existence.

She woke from a restless sleep as morning sunlight crept through her window, bathing the room in pink tinged with gold. Her room bore evidence of her personality. It wasn't generally this tidy either. Noelle was not one for organization. Her bits and bobs, ornamental figurines and comfortable clutter, sparkled in the dim sunlight as Noelle stretched her arms above her head and turned to survey the damage her sleepless night had done to her eyes.

The dressing table mirror seemed to mock her. Her hair stood up in every direction, and her nightdress hung from her shoulder in a lank, disappointed sort of way.

She heard a soft knock on the door. "Come in, Alice," she responded through a yawn. She heard the door open and shut as she slid out of bed and stretched high on her tiptoes. "I have no idea what I'll wear to the park today. Maybe the printed muslin? The one with the flowers?"

"I think that dress looks very lovely on you."

Noelle shrieked and spun around, yanking the downy comforter off the bed to cover herself. "Wallace!" she hissed. Her mind had deadpanned in panic. "You're not supposed to be in here! What will people think if they see you sneaking out of my bedroom at the crack of dawn?"

"Oh, come on, 'Elle." He sidled over to her as though he hadn't a care in the world and sank down onto her bed.

"Wallace Gerson," she seethed. "I insist that you..."

"Leave at once!" he finished her sentence calmly. "Quit being silly 'Elle. We used to do this all the time when we were children. Don't you remember the summer I spent here while my parents traveled to Paris?"

"When we were *children*, Wallace," said Noelle, her shoulders relaxing despite herself. "When we were young. You shouldn't be in here."

"You didn't used to care at all," he said, grinning as his eyes roved over her. "I used to sleep in here all the time, remember? And I'd creep back to my room at dawn."

"Because I was afraid of the dark," she sighed, sitting down on the corner of the bed, still wrapped in the coverlet.

"Yes, you were. You were afraid of all those things that go bump in the night," he whispered, "and from the looks of it," his warm brown eyes skated over her exhausted face. "You still are. Rough night?"

"Wallace, what are you doing in here?"

Her friend sat up from amidst her pillows, fixing her with a penetrating stare. "I owe you an apology," he said.

"What for?"

"For my behavior, last night. I didn't mean to come off as... strange. Things between us have never been strange. They've always been easy..." he drifted off and his eyes trailed down her body before finding hers again. "I don't want things between us to change," he whispered, finally. "I'm sorry that I left you alone with that architect. What's his name? I couldn't even tell if you wanted me to or not."

"Kenneth is a good man," said Noelle defensively. "I don't mind his company."

Something in Wallace's eyes hardened a fraction. "I see," he said. He swallowed roughly, and then he smiled with what seemed a great effort. "Anyways," he straightened and bent forward to plant a very familiar kiss on the top of her head. "I hope I didn't ruin the entire weekend with my awkwardness."

"Not at all. Although you may have ruined it with your apology," laughed Noelle. She tossed a pillow at him. "Now get out of my room before someone sees you."

Chapter Twelve

Kenneth was whistling softly under his breath as he slid out of his room. He had been informed last night that breakfast would be served at ten o'clock in the morning. His stomach gave a rumble. Ten o'clock? He was accustomed to waking at dawn and eating shortly after, even following a late night out. Ten o'clock was practically lunch time for him.

He wandered down the long hallway, doing his best to tread quietly so he wouldn't wake the other guests. He planned to locate the kitchens—something he wasn't entirely sure that he could accomplish given the vastness of the Brittlers' home—and proceed outside for a long walk in the garden with a snack in his hand. It was rare that he had a moment of free time and Kenneth liked to walk in the morning. He liked to listen to the birds awake and begin to sing. He was still humming cheerfully and about to turn down the steep steps that lead up from the lower floor when he caught movement out of the corner of his eye.

He stopped, peering down the hallway toward the door he had watched Noelle disappear into the night before. A dark-haired head had popped around the corner of the doorframe. As Kenneth watched, he saw it turn left and right, clearly checking to see if the coast was clear before slipping out of the door and straightening up. He swallowed past a hard lump in his throat. It was Gerson.

What was he doing slithering out of Noelle's bedroom at the crack of dawn? The obvious truth crushed down on him an instant later. He heard Noelle's soft voice echo through the still-open doorway. He watched as Gerson poked his head back around the door and answered, and then he shivered with fury as he heard Noelle give a quiet little laugh.

Gerson shut the door and turned, heading down the hallway with a smug grin etched on his face. He froze when he saw Kenneth. And then, suddenly, he smiled.

"Good morning, Mr. Blackmore," he said cheekily, and then, with a disgusting skip in his step, he proceeded down the hall, around the corner and out of sight.

Kenneth didn't move. He thought he might have forgotten how to breathe. He stood there in the sleepy silence of the Brittlers' elaborate home and struggled to remember how to function. Noelle hadn't seemed the type. And let alone with Gerson. He remembered the look on her face when he had pointed out Gerson's obvious infatuation with her. She hadn't looked pleased. If anything, she had looked shocked and a bit guilty. He had moved away from her, and then turned back to say something else, only to see her plodding back to her room, her head hanging low. He'd meant to apologize for his forwardness in the garden. He'd meant to apologize for causing her grief with her old friend, but he hadn't been able to open his mouth.

He'd lain awake, thinking over what he would say when he saw her at breakfast the next morning. He'd dreamed of her in his arms. Shamelessly, foolishly, he had allowed himself to hope after he'd held her. He had, for a moment, thought she might care for him just as much as he was beginning to care for her.

His heart lay shattered at his feet. What a fool he had been, to think that a woman like her would ever think of him as anything other than what he was. A baker. That was all he was. A lowly town baker with aspirations and dreams far beyond his reach.

Kenneth shuffled down the front steps and out through the front door, no longer hungry.

The cool morning breeze felt like the breath of life. He gulped lungful after lungful of fresh, dew-drenched air, and then strode off around the side of the house. Not the way he had gone last night, not into the gardens where he had held Noelle in his arms and tasted her lips. He needed to clear his head. He needed to think.

He had to be honest with himself. It had taken very little for Noelle and Cynthia to convince him that coming to the party was an opportunity that he couldn't afford to miss. Cynthia had gone on and one about a once in a lifetime chance, and Noelle, sweet Noelle, had done little more than bat her eye lashes. He had trailed after her like a fish on a line and now he was reaping his reward.

Kenneth fell onto a stone bench beneath an overhanging tree and stared morosely out at the town beneath him. The Brittlers estate was situated at a point slightly higher than the rest of Manhattan, as though to emphasize their difference.

He remembered Margaret Piper, the dress-maker's daughter, and he recalled defending Noelle against her words. "The Brittlers are rather interesting," she had said.

"But I'm afraid us commoners are nothing more than a way for them to pass the time."

Kenneth scraped a hand through his dark hair. He hadn't ever thought there was any truth in Margaret's jealous words, but now... Had he really been nothing more than an amusing way to pass the time?

"Ah! Another early-riser!" Kenneth jumped at the unfamiliar, jovial voice that sounded beside him. "Apologies," said the man, "I didn't mean to startle you."

Kenneth stared. Thomas Brittler pushed back the tails of his frock coat and settled himself down beside him, tugging a pipe from his pocket. Lodging it firmly in the corner of his mouth, he fished around for a packet of tobacco.

"My daughter, Noelle, she's very taken with you, it seems," he said, eyeing Kenneth and speaking out of the corner of his mouth as he packed his pipe.

"I don't really think she is, sir," said Kenneth. He couldn't help himself. His insides ached with Noelle's deception. He wasn't sure that he'd be able to face her.

Thomas Brittler looked taken aback. "Really?" he muttered. "That so?"

Kenneth nodded his head, doing his very best to pull himself together so that he would not look as miserable as he felt.

"Hmm," said Thomas. He sat back on the concrete bench and took a long pull on his pipe. "No offense, son," he declared after a moment, "but I think I know my daughter a bit better than you do."

Kenneth looked up at him. He opened his mouth and then closed it again, shaking his head.

"You see," Thomas continued, his eyes on the smoke now spiraling up from the many factory chimneys in the distance. "She has taken a liking to you, I can tell."

Kenneth laughed sourly, but stopped quickly as Noelle's father frowned at him. It was clear that the man wasn't accustomed to being contradicted.

"She wouldn't have invited you here if she didn't like you," he said. "The problem that we're going to have is that I don't. Like you, I mean."

A bitter smile crept over Kenneth's face, despite himself. Wanting to impress Noelle's family and friends seemed like a thing of the past. "And why is that?"

Thomas Brittler took another pull on his pipe and blew out two identical smoke rings. "I've friends in Ireland, son. Got 'em all over the place, to tell you the truth."

Kenneth's heart sank right down past its usual spot and lodged somewhere in his navel. He looked at Thomas Brittler and waited for the blow to fall.

"I've been doing some asking around, obviously. And you know what? None of them have heard of an architect called Kenneth Blackmore." He leaned forward on his knees and turned to face Kenneth. His expression had lost its friendly, warm smile. In its place was the face of a hardened businessman who had dragged himself up from the ground and gained acceptance amongst the wealthy and honored. Thomas Brittler looked mean as he gazed across the short distance between them.

"I'm not a fan of being lied to," he said. "So, here's what we're going to do. Either you tell me who you really are or..." he paused, shrugging, "you leave. Quietly, and without a fuss. I'll even make your excuses. Because if you've been lying to me, you've been lying to my daughter and that means you're not the sort of man I want her to be associating with."

"Leave? Just like that?"

"Is that what you'd like to do?" Thomas took his pipe out of his mouth.

"I don't know," said Kenneth. He sighed. "But, I haven't been lying to your daughter, sir," he muttered.

"She knew who I was. She even orchestrated the idea. I wouldn't have attempted to come here on my own."

Thomas nodded. "Funny thing," he said. "There wasn't a whisper of a Kenneth Blackmore, not from anyone I spoke to over these last few days. But you know," he tapped his pipe in the air in front of him. "There were a few mentions of a bakery in town on 6th avenue ran by a man called Kenneth Black." He let out a chuckle.

Kenneth frowned down at his shoes.

"You'll want to be choosing your fake name more carefully next time," Thomas Brittler chortled. He sounded good natured once more, and Kenneth was strongly reminded of Noelle and her mercurial moods. He looked up.

"I'm sorry that I deceived you, Mr. Brittler. I'll just go get my things and be on my way."

"What are you talking about?"

Kenneth had stood up, his neck hot and his manner defeated. "I assumed—."

"Never assume, son. Never assume." Thomas Brittler stood up too. He eyed Kenneth up and down. "I know my daughter," he said again. "She can be annoyingly persistent when it comes to getting what it is she's after. I don't imagine she gave you much of a choice on the matter, did she?"

Smiling, Kenneth shook his head.

"Well," said Thomas, slapping Kenneth on the back. "I'd hate for her to think I sent you away because of who you are. It's probably best if you stay until Sunday afternoon. You won't want to miss the fireworks." Then, with a crooked smile and a wink, Noelle's father strode away from him.

Kenneth opened his mouth to say something. Anything. But how could he explain? How could he ever tell Thomas Brittler that the reason he wanted to leave wasn't because he had been found out, but because his daughter had broken his heart.

Chapter Thirteen

Noelle smiled as she entered the dining room, where a magnificent breakfast was laid out on an array of dishes and platters. Most of her mother's guests were already seated around the table. She had run a little bit late because her hair had refused to agree with her.

Sarah-Jane raised a questioning eyebrow at her, but Noelle was distracted almost at once by Kenneth, who was sitting a few places away talking quietly with a flamboyantly dressed Amelia Gene Stovich and her husband. He looked drawn, as if he had seen some sort of great battle since she had last saw him

Amelia looked up, and spotting her, waved her over. Noelle moved to take the empty seat between her and Sarah-Jane, but was stopped by a small hand on her shoulder.

"Good morning, sister, have you missed me?"

Noelle gasped and then squealed in excitement as she spun around. "'Lottie!" She embraced Charlotte with such ferocity that her sister hiccupped.

"I've missed you too!" she laughed, recovering herself.

Sarah-Jane joined them, and then their mother and father. Everyone was hugging beautiful, red-haired Charlotte and shaking hands with her husband, Logan Drexel, welcoming them home

"You're just in time for breakfast," said Samantha. She looked excited, an emotion that was so very at odds with her usual stoic self that the sisters all exchanged glances. "Sit. Sit. Tell us about the Dakota Territory."

And now Charlotte's eyebrows had flown up. Their mother, who disapproved of nearly everything, in Noelle's opinion, had already voiced her distaste for what she had termed 'the rural life' several times over. None of the girls had expected her to show any interest in Charlotte's new home at all.

Flabbergasted, Charlotte followed their mother to the head of the table and sat down, eyeing her nervously, as though expecting her to shout: "April Fools!" at any given moment. Noelle frowned after them for a moment and then exchanged another look with Sarah-Jane.

"What's got in to her?"

"I don't know. It's a bit odd, isn't it? Just the other day, we sat down on the bed and had a conversation. Just like real people do."

Sarah-Jane laughed. "Let's go eat. We can ponder mother's strange personality crisis after breakfast.

Noelle looked around for her seat, and noticed Wallace eyeing her. In a very uncharacteristic way, he winked at her. Noelle raised her eyebrows at him, and he smiled and returned to his conversation with the gentleman next to him. As Noelle glided over to her seat, she spotted Kenneth, who, she was surprised to see, looked quite furious.

"What the matter?" she whispered in his ear on her way past him. She touched his shoulder lightly, concerned at his odd behavior, and felt him jerk away from her fingers. She frowned. He'd had absolutely no aversion to her touch the previous evening. But she could feel his fury, and it felt as though it had everything to do with her.

But she couldn't linger any longer. Kenneth's anger was evident on his face, and she noticed many people were watching them, including her father.

She moved away from him and sat down beside her elder sister, her smile wide and her eyes brimming with tears.

"I must have a word with you, my dear," said Amelia Gene Stovich, leaning forward and grasping Noelle's hand in hers.

"Oh?" said Noelle, doing her very best not to peer over Amelia's shoulder at Kenneth.

"Yes. Do you think you could inform the servants that my Ruby necklace has gone missing? You know. The one I was wearing last night."

"Missing?" Noelle finally felt secure enough to look her new friend in the eye. "Are you sure you haven't just misplaced it?"

Amelia looked troubled. "Yes, I'm certain of it. I always put it back in its little box every time I wear it. I set it out on the dresser last night and this morning, it wasn't there."

"How strange," muttered Noelle. "Has anyone been in your room?"

"Not that I'm aware of."

"I'll look into it at once," said Noelle.

She glanced over Amelia's shoulder at Kenneth, who refused to meet her eyes. Not that she really thought he would, but his behavior was very unusual. Did he have something to do with the theft?

After breakfast, Noelle excused herself and went to find Alice. Her lady was upstairs, changing the sheets in her parents' vast bedroom.

"Alice, dear, do you have a moment?"

Alice jumped. "Oh, Miss. What is it? Do you need your wrapper?" The girl looked terribly flustered.

"No..." said Noelle, slowly. "No, I wondered if you might inform the other girls that one of our guests has misplaced a rather expensive necklace of rubies. She's sure she had it last night, but now..." Noelle shrugged, noticing that Alice was looking highly distressed. "What is it, Alice?" she asked, worried.

Alice was twisting a pillowcase in her fingers, her brow creased with worry. "I'm afraid that's not the only thing that went missing last night, Miss," she said.

"Oh?"

"Some of the good silver is gone as well, and..." Alice's eyes filled suddenly with tears. "One of the gentlemen just had a terrible go at Athena. She's downstairs in the kitchen with Marcia, crying her eyes out, the poor thing. He said she'd stolen the buttons off his waistcoat. The big shiny ones, you know? He said he'd have her strung up for theft if she didn't give them back at once."

"Strung up for theft!" barked Noelle, outraged. "Are you sure he used those exact words?"

"Oh, yes, Miss. That's what made Athena so upset, you see. She doesn't have the buttons, and he said if she didn't return them by dinner, he would go to the constable."

"Well, surely he would have gone through father first, if he has an issue with a member of our household. And she wouldn't ever hang, Alice, don't fret. Father wouldn't allow that. Who is this man?"

Alice dabbed at her eyes. "It was Mr. Gerson, Miss."

"Wallace?"

"Yes, Miss."

Noelle frowned. "I'll have a word with him about how he treats our ladies." She said, flustered. "He's been acting very oddly lately; I'm not sure what's gotten in to him."

"Thank you, Miss," said Alice, bobbing her a little curtsy. "We'll do our very best to find out what has happened to the missing items. I know Mr. Hendrix wouldn't stand for a thief in the household. Only, when anything goes missing, folks always be thinking we're the ones to blame, Miss."

"Well, I'd trust you with my life, Alice, dear," said Noelle, and she kissed her lady on the cheek and scampered back downstairs to tell her father what was happening.

"Won't you ride alongside me today?"

It was Wallace and he was grinning again. Noelle frowned at him. "I want a word with you," she said, taking her friend by the arm and hauling him out into the hall.

"What's wrong?"

"Alice just told me that you terrified one of our ladies out of her wits. She said you accused her of thievery and threatened a hanging," Noelle hissed, taking a step back from him and eyeing him with resentment. "What kind of talk is that?"

Wallace's face flushed blotchily scarlet. "She took the coat away for washing and when she brought it back this morning, the gold buttons were all missing," he said. "What was I supposed to think?"

Noelle glared at him. "You could have tried to control your temper a bit," she said. "You should have gone to Father, or Hendrix. He'd have found out what happened at once."

"I..." he paused, surveying her furious expression. "I wasn't thinking," he finished. "That's the only riding jacket I brought with me, and now the buttons are all torn off it." He frowned and then his shoulders rose and fell in an irritable shrug. "Perhaps I overreacted a bit," he said. "I wanted to look my best for you this morning."

"Oh." Noelle couldn't think what else to say. She felt her anger fading as quickly as it had come.

Behind them, in the foyer, the front door was suddenly thrown open, and Noelle watched their many guests making their way outside to the line of waiting carriages.

Wallace placed a hand on the small of her back. "I'm sorry I overreacted. I seem to be apologizing for that quite a lot lately." He smiled sheepishly at her as they followed the others out into the yard. "So, will you ride with me?"

Noelle looked around. Kenneth passed just behind Wallace as he spoke and he cast her another furious glare. What on Earth had she done?

Offended and hurt by his behavior, she placed her hand in the one Wallace offered her. "Yes," she said, loudly enough so that Kenneth could hear her. "I'd love to."

Her mother had planned an afternoon outing. A picnic in Central Park, followed by a carriage parade along the pathways before the group returned home for supper and lawn games.

It was a brilliantly sunny day. Noelle had chosen to wear the floral-patterned muslin dress, but she couldn't decide if it was for her own reasons, or because Wallace had said that he thought she looked lovely in it. She could hardly decide what her feelings towards Wallace were anymore. It was as though Kenneth's obvious interest in her had awakened some dormant possessiveness in her old friend. He was certainly no longer hiding his interest in her, if he ever had been. Perhaps Noelle had merely begun paying attention.

But Kenneth's conduct towards her was unprecedented. He had always been so warm and genuine towards her and she couldn't stop raking over the things she had said and done, the kiss they had shared and everything in between, trying to interpret what atrocity she had committed that might have offended him so.

Wallace escorted her to the place where his carriage stood waiting in line with the others. "You look awfully cheerful this morning," Noelle commented, as he held her hand and assisted her into the chaise.

Wallace's grin widened. "Perhaps it was the sight of you this morning, all rosy cheeks and..." he winked, finishing on a whisper, "so delightfully exposed."

Noelle could have slapped him. Her face went from pale to pink in an instant. She held herself in check as he climbed into the carriage and settled himself down on the cushioned bench next to her. "I don't know what has gotten into you, Wallace Gerson," she hissed in his ear after a moment. "But it would do you good to remember that you are speaking to a lady. And I would remind you that your presence in my room this morning was not welcomed or anticipated."

Wallace flushed as he met her stern gaze. "I'm sorry, 'Elle," he whispered, and his hand reached out to stroke the back of hers in an apologetic, if rather intimate sort of way. "But you were quite beautiful in the early morning light. It's a sight I wouldn't mind seeing more of."

Noelle's heart leapt into her throat as the carriage set off. What was he saying? She swallowed before speaking again, choosing her words carefully.

"Well, if that's the case, Mr. Gerson, I'll not bother washing my face or combing my hair the next time you stop in for a chat."

He laughed and Noelle sighed with relief, glad he didn't press the issue.

She was quiet on the ride into town. It was noon and the other occupants in the line of carriages laughed and shouted, enjoying themselves, but Noelle couldn't seem to calm her mind. It kept returning to Kenneth, who she had noticed climbing into the chaise of Kendra and Arnold Forth just behind Wallace's. Her heart had stirred with a jealousy that she could not allow herself to feel as she had watched him take a seat beside the Forths' beautiful, young daughter.

What did it matter? Yes, she had been rather hoping to spend the day with Kenneth. Hoping that perhaps they might have a conversation about the rather *inappropriate*, blissful moment they had stolen in the garden last night. But clearly, she had done something wretchedly improper. She had offended him, somehow. Was she *that* bad at kissing? But no, that couldn't have been it. Was it her friendship with Wallace? And if it was... what right did Kenneth Black have to dictate with whom she was to spend her time? What was it to him?

Nothing. Because nothing could come of their attraction to one another. No. This was best. It didn't matter why he was angry with her. This distance was the best thing for them. She never should have invited him to come to the party in the first place. Resigned, and angry, Noelle allowed herself to relax into Wallace. Really... he was a good man. Why shouldn't she allow her old friend to court her if he was so inclined? They'd known one another so very long after all. It truly wasn't that far of a leap from friendship to courtship...

Chapter Fourteen

"So, you're in the cotton trade?"

"Yes, well," Mr. Forth cleared his throat. "For quite some time, now," he said, and for some reason, he glanced at his wife, who was smiling benignly at Kenneth from behind her fan.

"It's truly a lovely day for a picnic, don't you think Mr. Blackmore?"

The Forths' daughter, Kimberly, was trying her very best to recapture Kenneth's attention. She was a slight girl of a mere sixteen or seventeen years, and he couldn't quite think how she had managed to talk him into riding alongside her into the city. He'd seen red when he'd witnessed Gerson leading Noelle out of the parlor, where they had once again been ensconced *alone.* Could they not keep their hands off one another for five minutes?

Trying to rein in his temper, he'd agreed with the first thing anyone had said to him, and regretted it almost at once. Mr. and Mrs. Forth were looking at him with an intense curiosity. They looked somehow...hopeful, and Kenneth couldn't begin to fathom what advantage they sought to gain from his company.

"Do tell us about Spain," said Mrs. Forth. "I hear you were part of the construction of the Sagrada Familia. I can't believe it. It must have been fascinating to be part of a project like that."

Kenneth nodded, and found himself wishing for a drink. It was hardly noon, and already he was praying for the day to end so that he might hasten his departure the next day. He felt bad for ignoring the Forths, who were exchanging looks that told him they were all running out of ideas for engaging him in a conversation that he did not want to have.

"Won't you join me for a walk by the lake while we're at the park this afternoon?" asked the girl. She was shifting in her seat, leaning forward as though fascinated by his mere presence. He frowned at her, trying to think of an excuse, but when none came to mind he said:

"If you like," then returned to staring at the scenery as they passed by. People were jumping out of the streets as the procession of carriages passed. Some doffed their hats, others waved. Kenneth imagined that he would have been one of them were it not for Noelle. Her name kept echoing in his head. Kenneth could hardly remember a time when he had felt so miserable.

The carriages drew to a bumping, jingling halt just inside the park entrance, and Kenneth darted away from the Forth family as soon as he was able. He felt distinctly ruffled. Is this what it was like to be an eligible bachelor in high society? Parents doing their very best to shove their daughters down your throat? He chuckled dryly to himself. It wasn't so very different in the common world, he supposed. Margaret had been much the same. He thought, perhaps, that he might have been too hard on her.

It wasn't, after all, very easy to be lonely.

He tried not to watch Gerson as he assisted Noelle from his carriage. He tried not to notice the way she laughed at something the man said, or the way his insides burned, aching as though they had been filled with hot coals. He tried to ignore it all, all the while telling himself that there had never been cause for him to hope... But she had given him a cause. With her smiles. With her laughter.

With her... everything. He wondered if he had imagined it, and next he tried to convince himself that he had.

He struggled not to turn away from Noelle as she moved towards him through the crowd. "A word?" she asked, her voice cold.

He gave a sharp little nod and they stepped to the side to allow another group to pass them.

"I've been asked to make enquiries into some items that have gone missing during the night," she said. Her manner was curt. "Do you know anything about them? Have you seen anything odd?"

"Why would I know anything?" he snapped, and another furious thought entered his mind. "You think I stole them."

"I never said that!"

"You implied it," he hissed. "Is it not enough to watch me suffer? Must you confine me to prison for theft as well?"

Noelle's eyes widened. "What have I done to offend you, Kenneth?"

"I don't know," he growled. "Why don't you take a moment to think it over?" his eyes found Gerson's, watching their argument with a satisfied smirk behind Noelle's back.

Her shoulders slumped. For a moment, Kenneth almost felt bad. For a moment. Then he moved away from her, where he couldn't smell her or feel her warmth, and he felt as though he were moving away from the sun.

He watched out of the corner of his eye while she rejoined Gerson, his blood pounding in his temples, and then he turned and almost walked right into someone.

"Oh!" It was the Forth girl, she had tripped on the hem of her skirt in her rush to keep up with him and now grabbed his forearm to keep herself from falling.

"My dear, are you alright?" several women all chirped at the same time.

Kimberly laughed. "I'm fine, thank you. Thanks to Mr. Blackmore here!"

The ladies tittered and whispered behind their fans to one another.

"I'm afraid I can't say the same for my dress," moaned Kimberly.

Kenneth looked down at her hemline. A neat tear ran down the front; it looked as though the buckle of her shoe had caught.

Samantha Brittler approached them, eyeing Kenneth like a wrathful eagle. He wondered if her husband had mentioned the conversation he and Kenneth had had that morning.

She bent down and examined the tear in the Forth girl's dress. "Oh, this is nothing, dear, don't fuss. There's a fabulous dress-maker in town. We'll send one of the footmen for her at once and she'll have that mended in a trice."

"Oh, I would be ever so grateful," gushed Kimberly Forth. "Thank you so much, Mrs. Brittler."

"Don't mention it, my dear," said Samantha Brittler. She smiled woodenly at Kenneth. "Thank goodness Mr. Blackmore was here to save the day," she said, and then she turned and walked away.

"I'm so sorry, Mr. Blackmore. How dreadfully clumsy of me."

"Are you alright," asked Kenneth irritably. The girl had yet to release his forearm.

"Oh, my ankle does hurt a bit. Perhaps we could sit down?"

Kenneth sighed and looked around for a bench. He noticed Noelle watching him, and then an idea struck him.

His eyes on Noelle's, he scooped Kimberly Forth up into his arms and carried her to the nearest bench. She squealed with delight, looking around for her mother.

It wasn't particularly nice or particularly proper, but something in Kenneth had snapped in a spiteful, vindictive way. If Noelle didn't care for him at all, she wouldn't react. She wouldn't... Kenneth glanced up as he settled Kimberly down on the wooden bench. She was beaming up at him, but he was watching Noelle, who had turned and strode away from him as fast as she could go. Her back was ramrod straight, and she looked furious.

Satisfied, Kenneth set himself down on the bench beside Kimberly, ignoring the many giggles and whispers of their fellow picnickers. "Shall I call someone for you?" he asked solicitously.

"Oh, I think I'll be alright in a moment," sighed Kimberly.

"Very well," said Kenneth, and he started to get up. Now that Noelle was out of sight, he'd lost any interest he'd had in the girl's companionship. But she had grabbed at his jacket sleeve, clinging to him so tightly, he worried that she might tear the fabric.

"Oh, stay with me, won't you? I don't want to sit here all on my own."

Kenneth had to fight to urge to tell Kimberly Forth that if she didn't want to sit there she could walk her tiny little body over to the picnic area with everyone else. "Very well," he said with yet another sigh, and he sat back down, staring around the park grounds and avoiding eye contact with everyone in the vicinity.

Kimberly attempted more idle chit-chat, but Kenneth's one and two word responses finally began to irritate her and she began to talk about herself in the most annoying fashion. It took Kenneth all of ten seconds of listening to her prattle to discover that he had absolutely nothing in common with the girl. He stopped listening, and it wasn't until he heard a familiar voice issuing from right beside him that he started and looked up.

"Kenneth?! Well, what a surprise it is to see you here!"

He gulped. Margaret Piper was looking down at him with an irritatingly cheerful smile on her pallid lips.

He glared at her, darting anxious glances around to see if anyone nearby had heard her.

"What are you doing here, Margaret?" he asked sharply in an undertone. Kimberly Forth was watching their exchange with wide, interested eyes.

Margaret raised her eyebrows at him. "Not embarrassed of my acquaintance, I hope, Kenneth. We've been friends for such an awfully long t—."

"Quit it, Margaret. What do you want?"

Margaret dropped her playful manner. "Mother was with a customer when the Brittlers' footman came in and said that there was an urgent need for a dress-maker at Central Park this very moment, so she sent me instead."

That was when Kenneth noticed that Margaret was clutching a tartan sewing kit in her hands.

"I see," he said. "Well, hurry up with it then."

"How do you two..." Kimberly Forth was looking between Kenneth and Margaret in confusion.

"Margaret's mother is my sister's dress-maker," said Kenneth quickly, silencing Margaret with a look.

"Oh..." said Kimberly. "So, have you... known each other long...?"

Kenneth let out a growl of annoyance. "Too long," he said, and Margaret looked offended.

"Come now, Kenneth. I don't think you're being very fair," said Kimberly, obviously enjoying the sport of prying into his background.

If it would have been acceptable for Kenneth to growl at that moment, he would have. As it was, he ran his fingers through his hair in frustration, praying for patience.

Margaret gestured him over and sat down beside Kimberly, lifting the tear in her hemline into her lap so that she could inspect it. "Kenneth's sister and I became friends after she had been visiting my mother's shop for some time," she said. "He disapproves of our friendship," she mock-whispered to Kimberly. "He thinks I'm a bad influence on her."

"And are you?" giggled Kimberly.

Margaret laughed. "Of course, I am!" she said, and both the girls fell into raucous giggles. Kenneth had had enough. Standing up, he began pacing back and forth in front of the bench, waiting for Margaret to finish mending the tear.

"There," she said at long last, pulling out a tiny pear of sheers and snipping away a couple of loose threads. "Good as new," she said.

"Oh, thank you so much!" cried Kimberly.

"Can I have a private word with you?" Kenneth snarled. He waited impatiently for Margaret to pack away her things and say goodbye to Kimberly.

"I'll have to stop in on you and your mother before we head for home the day after tomorrow," said Kimberly.

"I look forward to it," Margaret promised as Kenneth practically dragged her away. "Really, Kenneth, was that necessary?" she griped when, moments later, Kenneth dragged her behind a thick clump of trees.

"Necessary?" he hissed, disgusted. "You know why I'm here. You know that I'd be ruined if anyone found out who I really am. My business would be in shambles."

"Oh, Kenneth, sneaking into a glamorous party is hardly a crime," she said. "Must you always over exaggerate? How's it going? Where is our darling little debutante?"

"Don't talk about her like that," he snapped.

"Oh, Kenneth. Why the quick temper? This is so exciting!"

Kenneth glared at her. "Can you please leave?" he asked. "So that I might retain whatever scraps of my dignity I have left?"

Margaret crossed her arms, fuming. "I'm hardly doing any harm," she said. "I'd like to stay for a bit at least..."

"No," he said, bluntly. "Please leave."

"Well, I don't see why you should get to have all the fun." Margaret's voice had gone quiet, and Kenneth tensed. "What would your new friends think of you if I told them all who you *really* are?" she poked him in the chest. "I think the papers might pay a pretty penny to hear this sort of story."

"Margaret, I am begging you. I can't *do* this today." Kenneth shoved his fingers through his hair again, and

Margaret took a step back from him, surveying him coldly, her arms crossed over her chest.

"She did it, didn't she?" she asked quietly.

"Who? Did what?" he snapped, staring at her.

"Noelle. She got bored with you," she stated. Her eyes were roving over his. Kenneth supposed that he looked quite mad.

He threw his arms up into the air. "I don't know!" he cried, his voice tearing. "I don't know what I did. I don't know why she chose me… I was nobody and no one… and now…" he trailed off, his chest heaving. "I need you to leave, Margaret, please. Just let me get through the next couple of days and then I can go home. It will be as if none of this ever happened."

Margaret was looking at him sadly, her shoulders slumped. She didn't appear as though she was angry anymore. She exhaled heavily, and then reached up and gave his shoulder a squeeze. "No… it won't," she whispered. Then she hefted her sewing kit more securely onto her hip and departed, leaving Kenneth feeling hollow, and somehow… even worse than he had felt before she had come.

As Kenneth stepped out of the trees a few moments later, he almost ran smack into Wallace Gerson. He steadied himself by seizing the smaller man by his shoulders.

"Where is she? Is she with you?" Gerson looked uncomfortable facing Kenneth, but he also looked worried.

"Who?" Kenneth asked, flummoxed.

"Noelle!" exclaimed Gerson, flinging his hands into the air. "I heard you talking to someone. Noelle!" he shouted over Kenneth's shoulder into the trees.

"Why would she be with me?" snapped Kenneth. "She's your..." Kenneth didn't know how to categorize Noelle and Gerson's relationship in a way that wouldn't sound insulting.

"She's not with you?" Gerson appeared to be deflating before Kenneth's eyes.

"No."

"I can't find her," said Gerson. "She vanished almost as soon as we got here. I thought..."

Kenneth snapped to attention. "Wait. How long has it been since you've seen her?" he asked, his eyes scanning the crowds of people milling about in the park.

"A few hours," said Gerson. "She missed lunch, and I thought maybe it was because she found out that... that I... I thought maybe you might have mentioned our..."

The truth donned on Kenneth so suddenly that he took a step backward to gain his balance. "You let me think that you and Noelle were—."

"Yes, yes," grumbled Gerson, waving his hands dismissively. "I went to her room to apologize for my behavior the previous night, but nothing happened between us. She's too… Well, I wouldn't ever…" He swallowed, evidently in great discomfort.

"We have to find her," said Kenneth. He was furious at Gerson. He wanted to toss the boy on the ground and pummel him for a few moments, but that would have to wait. No one besides him knew the sort of danger that Noelle might be in right now. He began to stride towards the carriages, but at that moment, Noelle's footman came galumphing through the grounds toward them.

"Mr. Black," he said, clutching at a stitch in his side. "Mr. Black, I have to tell you something."

"Does her father know?" was all Kenneth had to say, and Kincaid shook his head.

Gerson was frowning. "Know what? What's going on? Look, she probably just tired of the gathering and headed for home. She wasn't acting as though she felt all that well on the ride over."

"Yes, I'm sure she went right home," said Kenneth sarcastically. "Why don't you go check?"

"Right-O," said Gerson, and he darted away to the line of carriages.

"That boy is thicker than a concussed mule," said Kincaid. "I'm her footman and she came in *his* carriage. How in the world would she have got home?"

Kenneth shrugged and broke into a run. "At least that gets him out from under our feet. Am I to understand that she told you the full story?"

Kincaid had fallen into step beside him. "About Jeb Dillard? Yeah, I been trying to keep an eye out for her," said Kincaid, nodding frantically, "but I lost her in the crowds. I looked everywhere, sir. I think it's time we tell someone what's happening."

Kenneth nodded. "Let's find Thomas."

Chapter Fifteen

Noelle awoke in darkness with her head throbbing, fit to burst. Her surroundings came into focus so slowly that she began to worry that her eyes had been effected in some sort of accident.

She was lying in the dirt, in some dark, low-ceilinged place. Every breath she inhaled felt thick with dust. She gave a little cough, and that was when she noticed her hands were bound. Thick, course rope encased her wrists, wound so tightly that she couldn't feel her fingers. The muscles in her arms ached from being suspended above her head, and her hair was caked with grime.

Where was she? What had happened to her? The last thing she remembered was watching Kenneth Black lift the Forths' daughter and carry her away. He'd been smirking at her the whole time, as though enjoying every moment of her discomfort, and she'd turned around and stomped away... she'd gone... where had she gone? It was all so muddled. She'd wanted to be alone, to think, so she had strolled up the path, away from the group... Away from her mother, her father and Kincaid. Away from safety.

Jeb.

The terror had set in now. It was a corrosive, debilitating thing. The faster her heart raced, the faster she breathed, and there wasn't enough air here. Not enough air.

"Help me!" she screamed, so loud her lungs felt as though they were ripping themselves into bits. "Someone!! Please!! Help me!" She fought the ropes binding her, but they wouldn't give an inch.

She remembered now. She remembered it all. A hand had grabbed her around the waist and lifted her bodily from the ground. She had been thrown against a tree and her face had been covered with a cloth. It had smelled clinical and overpowering, and she'd tried to shove it away, tried to fight back, to scream, and he had laughed.

She knew that laugh. It had haunted her nightmares for weeks, despite her best efforts to reassure herself that she was quite alright, that she was safe. And then the note had come, because he'd wanted to scare her. He'd wanted to punish her for stealing everything from him. He'd wanted her to know that he was watching her.

Heavy footfalls sounded above her head, and Noelle fell silent, trying to listen over her pounding heart. She could make out the rumble of two voices, both male, but one lifted in anxiety.

"We shouldn't have done this."

"Would you quit yer sniveling?" The second man's voice sent a fresh shiver of terror sliding down Noelle's spine, but along with the fear came a wave of fury like nothing she'd ever felt before. It *was* him. Jeb. "If we stick to the plan, no one need ever know who we were."

"This is blackmail, Dillard."

"Yeah, and you won't be complaining when we get a nice, fat pay off, will you?"

"If we're caught—."

"The only way we'll be caught is if you can't keep your trap shut and stick to the plan."

"But—."

"It's done, Pruette. We have the girl. We just give them a little time to worry for her, then we get the money, we ditch the girl. Simple. Easy. We get outta town... no one is ever the wiser."

Jeb's partner cleared his throat. "Fine. Fine. But Dillard... this is the last time. I'm going straight after this."

"Whatever you say, boss," laughed Jeb.

Noelle shivered. So, she had been kidnapped. They were holding her for a ransom. A ransom they would likely receive... Noelle knew that her father would do anything to get her back. Oh, why hadn't she told him? If he'd have known of Jeb Dillard, Noelle was sure that her father would have hired an endless stream of investigators to find him and bring him to justice. But... she'd been thinking of poor Kincaid. He would have lost his position with the family if she had told her father what had happened to her... She couldn't allow that, it hadn't been his fault at all.

But now, Noelle realized that this kindness might cost her her life. "Ditch the girl," they had said. What did that mean? Noelle couldn't fight the terrifying images swarming through her mind. She had very little hope that she was going to come out of this alive.

Her wrists throbbed with pain, her blood pulsing in a spasmodic rhythm through her cinched veins. The air was pressing on her from all sides. She couldn't breathe. She couldn't think, and she was going to die.

No.

The voice in her head was strong and clear. Determined.

No. You are not going to die. Not like this. Not trapped like an animal in a dismal gray cellar. Use your sense, girl.

Noelle straightened up, swallowing hard through a throat that felt as dry as parchment.

Think, the voice said. *THINK.*

She examined her gloomy surroundings. Shafts of light slid through the boards of the flooring overhead in periodic intervals. Around her, she could hear a steady chugging that sounded like massive machines at work. Where is this place? Something about the sound was familiar, but Noelle couldn't understand why. She was lying in a mess of dirt and rubble beneath the floor of a warehouse? Or perhaps, a shop? Her wrists were pinioned above her head, and her body felt weak.

Screaming her lungs out wouldn't help. Her screams had had no effect on her captors. She was sure they had heard her. Evidently, they weren't concerned that anyone would be able to make them out over the constant noise of the machines around them. They'd chosen this spot well, perhaps tested it with their own shouts to judge whether it would work for their nefarious plans.

Help. Help. Help.

But no one would know where to start looking. She felt as though she had been unconscious for hours. Surely her family would have noticed her absence by now. Would Kincaid tell them about Jeb? She hoped he would. But if he didn't... Would Kenneth? He might. He was an intelligent man. Noelle only hoped that whatever offense she had committed in his eyes was not enough to stop him from trying to help her. But the way he had looked at her this morning. With such contempt and such... pain. It was as though she had mortally injured him somehow. But what could she have done over the one night that they had been apart?

The answer came to her then. Sharp in the dullness of her fogged mind.

He *must* have seen Wallace exiting her chambers that morning. Must have thought that she and Wallace were together through the night. She nearly laughed aloud with the uselessness of it all. These minor discrepancies that had caused her so much pain, they were all a long way off, hidden in some former life. One thing existed now. One. Her life was in danger and *she* was the only one that could save her now.

She needed to try to escape. But how could she do it? Her hands were bound so tightly.

She shifted around trying to peer up at her wrists through the darkness. The rope holding her had been wound around a short beam that held up the floor above. Behind her was nothing but a solid wall of brick. She was tucked away beneath the floor of some massive building... The darkness around her, separated by the narrow strips of light, stretched as far as she could see in either direction. Even sitting, as she was, the boards that made up the floor of the space above her were only inches above her head.

If she could find a way to get free, she might be able to crawl away from the place where Jeb and his accomplice paced and find another exit.

She looked around for something sharp near her wrists... anything that she could use to weaken her bonds.

"It's time." It was Jeb's voice, and Noelle watched the dust fall where his boots clomped against the floorboards as he moved across the room. "I'll make my way through town and send a messenger to the Brittlers. You stay here and keep an eye on the girl." Noelle couldn't hear the other man's low response, but Jeb laughed. "I'll take care of it when I return. Just keep an eye out."

His heavy footsteps pounded away across the floor, and Noelle winced against a deluge of grime as Jeb's hulking shadow passed overhead. She heard a door open and close, then there was silence but for the gears turning around her.

There was little time left.

Noelle let her head fall back against the ropes binding her and closed her burning eyes. She stretched her neck to the right and then the left, trying to ease her discomfort, and then she froze. There, against the back of her head, what was that? Something had pricked the skin there.

Pulling her body into a crescent so that she could squint behind her, Noelle spotted a patch of rough, unhewn timber. A nail protruded sideways from the beam. She stared at it, then hauled herself around as best she could and began hacking at the ropes holding her wrists. She began to sweat, and the numbness began creeping up her arms, but she daren't stop. Not even when she heard the tell-tale sound of Jeb's boots returning. Not even when she knew it was almost too late.

Chapter Sixteen

Kenneth could hear the blood rushing in his ears. He was awash in guilt and fury; they alternated their onslaughts on his mind like waves tossed onto the deck of a ship in a wild storm. It was his fault. This was all his fault.

If he hadn't gotten so caught up in his own misery that he'd forgotten to keep watch, to stand guard. He had *known* in his heart that Jeb Dillard was still lurking around. How could he have been so careless? Even for all his anger at her for the things he had thought she had done, he *never* should have allowed her out of his sight when they were away from the safety of her home. What had he been thinking?

Thomas Brittler paced before him, barking out orders to servants and guests alike. The man's face was a mask of anxiety and fury.

"Why?!" he shouted at Kenneth for what felt like the fiftieth time. "Why wasn't I informed?"

"I assumed Dillard would come after me," muttered Kenneth. "I didn't expect him to be so bold. I spoke to the authorities, and they assured me they were on the lookout for him. I checked back every day, and when there hadn't been any sign, they told me they thought he'd left town."

Thomas Brittler glared between him and Kincaid. "I would have found him. You think I'd let a man attack my daughter and get away with it?" He pounded his fist on the table. "I still can't understand why she didn't tell me what happened!"

Kincaid shifted his feet guiltily. "Sir, I'm afraid that Miss Noelle was trying to protect me."

"Protect you?"

"She..." he hesitated. "She was trying to protect my position, sir. She was also... a bit embarrassed, I think, sir. She said something about bringing a scandal down on the family just before the party."

Thomas Brittler laughed bitterly. "That does sound like her," he said.

"Mr. Brittler, the constable has arrived to see you. He's brought the investigator." The footman who had delivered the message withdrew quickly as a portly man dressed all in black shoved his way into the room, a gleaming badge pinned to his shirtfront. He was followed by a second, more subdued man, who looked around the room with an air of inquisitive intelligence.

"Mr. Johnathon Groon at you service, sir!" said the constable, affecting a sharp salute. "And this is Mr. Dower."

Mr. Dower did not salute Thomas Brittler. He strode forward and shook his hand in the solemn way one might greet the bereft at a large funeral. "I'm sorry to hear about your daughter, Mr. Brittler, sir. You have reason to believe that she is in danger?"

"My daughter is missing, Mr. Dower. I'd say she's in plenty of danger."

"Mmhmm. Mmhmm." Mr. Dower took out a notepad and pencil. "When was she last spotted?"

"About seven hours ago," interrupted Kenneth, striding forward. "Mr. Dower, I think I know who might have taken her."

The constable shifted his feet, eyeing Kenneth nervously. Kenneth could tell that Mr. Groon recognized him from his frequent visits downtown.

Mr. Dower fixed him with a wide, interested gaze. "Do tell," he said.

Kenneth launched into the story, starting at the very beginning when he had saved Noelle from Jeb, up until the moment she disappeared.

"So, you've seen this Jeb hanging around town?" asked Mr. Dower. "What makes you think he would really go so far to exact revenge?"

Kenneth wanted to take hold of the man and shaken him. "He has motive, sir."

"Has he made any threats towards her since his err... citizen's arrest took place?"

"I..." Kenneth paused. He had no idea.

Kincaid stood up. "She did receive a message from the man, Mr. Dower."

"A message? What sort of message?"

"It said 'Found you pretty girl,'" he whispered.

Mr. Dower looked between them all slowly. From Thomas Brittler, who was looking furious and rather terrified, to Kincaid, who looked as though he was going to be sick. When his gaze finally came to rest on Kenneth, he said: "Do you have any proof that this man has in fact, kidnapped Miss Brittler?"

"There seems to be enough proof to merit an investigation in the very least!" barked Thomas.

"Father?" Noelle's sisters had opened the door and shoved their way into the room. The hallway outside Thomas Brittler's office was thronging with curious guests.

"Thomas?" Samantha Brittler was just behind them.

"Close the doors, quickly," he said to the three of them.

They did so and Sarah-Jane turned back to face him.

"Father, what's going on? Where's Noelle. Who is..." she stopped when she saw the badge shining on the constable's chest.

"What is going on?" asked Samantha, rushing to her husband's side.

"Mr. Brittler," it was Mr. Dower speaking, his voice no louder than it had been a moment before. "I'm afraid that without conclusive proof, there is very little I can do to help you. Your daughter has only been missing for a handful of hours. There is no evidence at all of foul play."

"No evidence?!" shouted Thomas, losing his head completely. He was sweating, and his eyes were wide. "Mr. Dower, if you do not find my daughter I will tear the very earth out from beneath your feet. Do you wish to test my reach, sir? Because I assure you, that if you refuse to help my family, I will do *everything* in my power to *destroy* everything you hold dear."

Sarah-Jane and Charlotte were looking at their father as though they had never seen him properly before. Samantha placed a bracing palm against her husband's chest.

Mr. Dower had fixed Thomas with a penetrating stare. "I will do all in *my* power to find her, sir," he said. His expression had remained completely blank as Thomas Brittler's voice rose, and he did not look as though this proclamation had had any effect on him whatsoever. He tugged his jacket straight. "I shall contact your family the instant I find anything," he said, and then he left, opening the office door and sliding out into the crowd of guests who were craning their necks to see inside.

When the door closed, the group exchanged uncomfortable looks. The constable shuffled from foot to foot, his coat pushed back and his hands deep in his pockets. Thomas Brittler looked at him.

"I've had my men searching for Dillard since Mr. Black came to me with the story," he said. "I'll redouble the efforts and tell them to keep an eye out for Miss Brittler as well." He shook Thomas's hand, and then he followed the investigator out of the room, shutting the door behind him.

"Is this about the thefts?!" Kenneth heard one of the guests ask the constable. "What's going on?!" shouted another.

"I don't know anything about Jeb Dillard," said Kenneth as the door closed. "I spoke to a few men at the factory where he used to work. They said they hadn't seen him since he was taken away."

Thomas opened his mouth to respond, and then he stopped. For a moment, he looked as though he was choking. His face went red, his tongue lolling, then he clutched at his chest and dropped like a stone.

"Thomas! Thomas!" Samantha shouted. She fell to the ground beside her husband. "Get the doctor. Someone call for the doctor!!"

Kincaid darted out into the hall.

"Thomas?!"

"Father!!"

Kenneth stared, and then he leapt into action. "Back away, give him some air. Mr. Brittler, can you hear me?"

Thomas Brittler's eyes fluttered.

"Mr. Brittler?"

"I'm alright," he said, groggily. "Samantha, my dear. I love you, but you're going to sever my fingers."

Samantha did not smile as she loosened her grip on her husband's hand. "Thomas," she pressed a worried hand to his forehead.

"I'm alright," he repeated.

"Let's get him over to the couch," said Charlotte.

Kincaid reentered the room, followed by a harassed looking man in a neat black suit.

"Mr. Brittler," he said sternly, coming up short. "I can't say that I'm pleased to see you."

"Well, I don't care much for you, either, Robert," said Thomas Brittler, chuckling. But he ruined the effect of the joke by wincing slightly.

Kenneth sat stunned in a chair beside Noelle's father. In the distance, he heard a factory whistle sounding, and he looked around.

"I can't sit here," he said apologetically. "I have to look for her."

Thomas nodded. "I'll come with you," he said, sitting up.

"Mr. Brittler, I must insist—." The doctor moved forward.

"You get back away from me, you old kook," said Thomas, holding out his hands. "If you think that you're keeping me here on this couch, you have another thing coming to you."

"Thomas, someone has to pacify the guests," said Samantha, soothingly. "Think. It could be all over the papers. We need an excuse."

Kenneth could tell that she was trying to give him a purpose, a reason to stay, but he could also tell that Noelle's father wasn't about to be deterred.

"I'll give them an excuse," growled Thomas, hauling himself to his feet. "Tell them that I think they're all insufferable busy-bodies and to go home." He took a step and then let out a low groan as his knees gave way.

Kenneth reached forward to catch the man under his arms. "Mr. Brittler, sir," he gasped, helping him back onto the couch. "I won't rest until I find her. Please, sir. Stay here."

Thomas Brittler was huffing. His chest was heaving and sweat glistened all over his face. He took hold of Kenneth's shirt front as he made to move away, and although the man was weak, his grip was strong.

"You bring her back to me, boy," he said. "Bring her back to me," and then he fainted with his fist still knotted in Kenneth's shirt.

"Move aside! Move aside," the doctor shoved himself forward, opening his bag.

Samantha Brittler seized Kenneth's arm as he ran past her. "Take the footmen. Take everyone. Send out a search party. Please," her eyes were full of tears. "Please find my daughter."

Kenneth nodded, feeling as though there was a lump the size of a gutty trapped in his throat.

He found Kincaid outside the Brittlers' home, walking up and down the long drive in the dark with a lit cigarette in his hand.

"Recruit as many men as you can," he said. "Let's go."

"Where will we start, Mr. Black?"

Kenneth shook his head as he moved toward the livery, "At the beginning," he said. And again, in the distance, a factory whistle beckoned.

Chapter Seventeen

Noelle felt the rope around her wrist give a little more as she listened to Jeb's huge feet thud across the floor overhead. She held her breath as the dust cloud descended and continued to saw at the ropes around her wrist.

"Is she coming?" it was Pruette's voice.

"Shut up," muttered Jeb.

"I want to know. She said she'd be here."

"I said shut up."

Pruette fell silent as Jeb continued to pace.

They must be waiting for someone to come with the money, Noelle thought. She scrubbed the sweat from her brow with her shoulder. Her fingers were tingling as the blood began to leak back into her hands. The rope gave a little more.

"You checked on the girl?" Jeb's voice asked.

"What for?" snapped the other man defiantly. "She ain't goin' anywhere."

Jeb let out a growl of frustration and Noelle saw his shadow move across the floor to the place where she lay. She knew he was peering down through the cracks in the floor, so she sat very still, hiding her wrists from view, her eyes turning up defiantly.

"You won't get away with this," she hissed, and her voice was rough from the dust and the chemical he had used on her. Her throat felt as though she had swallowed something vile and poisonous.

Jeb laughed. "Oh, sweetheart," he said through the gaps. "We already have."

Noelle felt tears pricking the corners of her eyes as Jeb moved away from her. Blessing the noise of the machines, she began to saw at the rope once more. Her movements were vigorous. She was almost free.

The nail slipped off the rope, slicing painfully into Noelle's wrist and she let out an involuntary squeak, and then she held her breath, looking up through the floorboards to see if Jeb had heard her. But she was so close now. The rope was almost completely severed. She stared up, petrified, waiting for the men to speak to one another, but there was nothing but silence. She began to saw once more. Almost... *there!*

The rope snapped, and Noelle wiggled her wrists back and forth frantically, fighting to free herself.

Suddenly, above her head, the floor shifted. Lantern light filtered through the clouds of dust, illuminating the place where Noelle sat, terrified, tugging at the ropes.

Jeb Dillard let out a vehement exclamation. "Pruette!" he shouted, and then he dived into the hole in the floor just as Noelle managed to scuttle sideways into the darkness. She was crawling on her hands and knees with absolutely no idea where she was going. The shadows were illuminated in slanting shafts of dim light. She heard Jeb screaming for Pruette just behind her and then felt a thick hand wrap around her ankle. Noelle screamed and kicked out hard. She felt her foot make contact with something solid and heard a grunt of pain, followed by a curse. But Jeb still had hold of her.

She kicked out again, but he was dragging her backward as she screamed, scrambling, fighting tooth and nail to free herself. She turned, and got a good look at Jeb's face as he struggled to keep a firm grip on her. His eyes were ringed in black bruises. On seeing this, Noelle aimed a solid kick right into the man's nose. She heard a crack and Jeb's hands released her as he howled with pain and rage.

Noelle hastened away into the shadows, crawling past beams and shafts of light into the blackest black, where she couldn't even see her own hand in front of her face. She could still hear Jeb and Pruette shouting. Moving as fast as she could on her hands and knees, she turned to see what was happening behind her. There wasn't much to see. She'd managed to get several yards away from where she had been bound. Through the square of light that was the patch of missing boards, she saw the hulking, crouched form of Jeb, gesticulating wildly to his accomplice. A moment later, Jeb stood up and his legs vanished as he climbed out of the hole and a skinnier man replaced him.

A heavy gas lamp in his hand, Pruette began skittering after her like some horrid three-legged creature of the darkness. Noelle darted this way and that, trying to lose him in the maze of beams and foundation and pipes. Heaving lungfuls of disgusting, chalky air, she turned another corner haphazardly and found she had come full circle. She could see the light filtering in through the hole in the floor up ahead. Her heart was pounding in her sore head and she paused, glancing over her shoulder. Pruette was nowhere in sight, but ahead, she could just make out the sound of raised voices. She crept closer.

"Why was she even under there in the first place!" this voice was a woman's, and Noelle's eyes widened in the gloom as she realized who it was.

"It seemed a safe enough place to keep her. She can't get out of there," Jeb growled. His voice sounded choked and Noelle could tell that he was speaking through a heavy nose bleed.

"This factory is enormous!" shouted the woman. "How are you planning to search every nook and cranny beneath the floor before the workers arrive at dawn?"

Noelle couldn't make sense of what she was hearing. Why would she be involved in this?

"Gotcha!" Noelle screamed as Pruette leapt on top of her, pinning her to the dirt. She struggled, kicking out, but the man had her sore wrists in his hands once more and he forced her face into the dirt as retrieved another rope from nowhere and began tying it around her wrists. "I'm sorry," he whispered in her ear, "this will all be over soon. We'll have you home real soon."

Noelle jerked her head backward and both she and Pruette screamed in pain as their skulls collided. "Get off of me!!!" she screeched.

Just then, something changed. There was a heavy grinding of gears and the high screech of metal on metal and all around them, the chugging machines fell slowly silent.

"You got her, Pruette?" came Jeb's thick voice, much quieter now.

"Yeah, I got her," Pruette moaned. He climbed off Noelle and tugged her forward, making her fall face-first into the dirt once more. She yanked at the cords binding her wrists, but Pruette was stronger than he looked.

She cried then. She broke down and cried, and she called out to the woman standing on the floor above. She said her name and she begged her for help.

After a few moments, despite her best effort, Noelle was dragged into the open square of light.

"Well, well, well," said the woman's voice. "Not so pretty and perfect now, are we, Miss Brittler?"

And Noelle looked up into Cynthia's face.

"I don't understand," she whispered. She could feel tears tracking down her dirt-smattered cheeks. "Why?"

Cynthia let out a high, cold laugh. She looked nothing like the sweet, cheerful pixie of a girl Noelle had first met all those weeks ago. Gone was the pleasant, friendly smile.

It had been replaced by an ugly look of loathing and distain.

"Why?" she asked mockingly. "Come up here out of the dirt, Miss Brittler, and you know what? I'll tell you why."

Pruette shoved Noelle, and Jeb seized her by the hair, forcing her above ground. Noelle's face was screwed up against the pain as Jeb yanked her into the center of the room and sat her down on a nearby barrel. Noelle looked around. She was in some sort of factory store room.

"It wasn't supposed to be this way, Noelle," said Cynthia. She was watching her with wide, innocent eyes. "My brother and I, we were supposed to move forward. We were supposed to be a team."

Noelle scrubbed her hands over her eyes, which were burning in the light after becoming so accustomed to the darkness.

"I always wanted just a little more," she said. "An apartment in town would be nice, maybe a room that was big enough to turn around in. Not too much, just a change, you know.

"We started at rock bottom, Kenneth and me. Our parents left us *nothing*. We had to make our own way. When we started the bakery, I thought it was the beginning of a new life for us, but..." she sighed. "It didn't really work out that way, did it? You know, I don't particularly like baking. Kenneth always told me that this would be temporary. He said once we had the money, he would hire a few hands to help run it. I thought, maybe, just maybe we were almost there. But he was so..." she ended this word on a groan, "content."

Noelle was incredulous. "This is about the bakery?" she asked, staring at Cynthia in disbelief.

"It's not about the bakery, you stupid girl," hissed Cynthia. "It's not about the bakery or my brother or any of it. It's about... you."

"Me?"

"Yes, you. Your family, your money. You wave your good fortune in other's faces as though you are so much better than us. You never realize what it does to the people who *die a little* just to make due." Cynthia scraped a hand through her hair, just like Noelle had seen her brother do on many occasions. "We bend over backwards, day in and day out, smiling and making *other people* as happy as we can manage to make them. Who is the last person you made happy besides yourself?"

"That would be me."

Everyone in the room turned to face the doorway as the door swung open and slammed against the opposite wall. Kenneth stood there, and his expression was murderous. Jeb and Pruette moved forward but Cynthia held up her hand to stop them.

"Did you come alone?"

Noelle frowned, terrified. She glanced between Kenneth and Cynthia, scared to hear the words that she thought she might. That he had been in on this. That he had help orchestrate her kidnapping. She didn't think her heart could take it.

"I have a group of six or seven men with me," he said. "Let her go, Cynthia."

"I can't do that," snapped Cynthia, and Noelle heard the click of a barrel just behind her head. "This wasn't supposed to happen," she whispered. "She wasn't supposed to know I was here. I thought you'd save her. I already gave the papers the story. I thought if you saved her... you would become a legend. The man who *saved* Noelle Brittler's life. They would have rewarded you, and we could have made something of ourselves."

"You think so?" said Kenneth, his voice was calm. He took a step forward.

Cynthia nodded and then pointed the gun at him. “Please don’t come any closer, Ken.”

“What made you change your mind?” asked Noelle. She turned in her seat to see Cynthia’s hand shaking as she pointed a gun directly between Noelle’s eyes.

“You heard my voice,” Cynthia whispered. “I had no idea you were so close. I only came in because Jeb came to tell me you’d escaped. But then we were shouting and the machines shut down and we heard you and Pruette... you said my name...” she whispered the last sentence, and her voice was heavy with remorse. “You said my name.”

Noelle turned away from Cynthia and knew that the bullet was coming. Her eyes found Kenneth and she stared at him. He was so very handsome, and for that split second of a moment, Noelle knew that even given the choice, he was the last thing she ever wanted to see.

“Cynthia,” Kenneth was speaking, and Noelle was watching his lips move. “Cynthia, stop. I won’t protect you. I won’t.”

Noelle’s eyes found the tear streaks on Cynthia’s face. They glistened in the light from the lamp in Pruette’s hand.

“If you do this,” whispered Kenneth, “I won’t stand beside you. I’ll turn you in.”

"I'll drag you down with me!" sobbed Cynthia.

Kenneth took a step closer to his sister, his hand outstretched. "Then I'll hang for your crimes," he said. "Is that the life you wanted for us?"

Cynthia's hand was still shaking, Noelle watched her finger twitch on the trigger.

"There's no coming back from this," Kenneth whispered. "Cynthia, put the gun down."

Cynthia stared at her brother, and little by little, Noelle saw the gun dropping. Kenneth covered the distance between them in two long strides, and in a second, the gun was in his hand. Cynthia collapsed into him, sobbing uncontrollably into his shoulder as his eyes met Noelle's. He nodded toward the door.

Kincaid stepped into the store room, followed by four other armed men. They kept their weapons focused on Jeb and Pruette as Kincaid darted to her side.

"I've got you, Miss. Everything is going to be alright. Come on, let's get you home."

Chapter Eighteen

The guests were packing. Noelle was in the library with her father, her head on his knee as he read to her out of the tattered Bible he'd had since he was a boy. The sound of his voice was familiar, and soothing. It was good to hear it, even if he sounded weak with exhaustion.

Noelle was drained. She felt as though she had been wrung out and left to dry in the hot sun. It was several moments before she realized that her father was no longer speaking. He had fallen asleep as he read, and was snoring gently. Noelle took his Bible from him and closed it.

The doctor had said that her father was likely to make a full recovery if he followed the instructions that he had left for him. The list went something like: no smoking, no alcohol, no excess strain, plenty of rest. So, he wanted father to stop doing the things he loved to do and add in things that he couldn't stand. Thomas Brittler was not one for "resting."

There was a soft knock on the door. It was her mother. She poked her head around the library door and smiled at the sight that greeted her.

"Resting," whispered Noelle with a grin, and she tip-toed out the door.

Her mother embraced her. She'd been doing this every time she saw her for the past day, and when she pulled away, her eyes were swimming with tears.

"Mother, don't cry," sighed Noelle. "Look at me. I'm quite alright."

"I can't believe you thought you had to endure an attack like that all on your own. You should have told me."

"But Dillard didn't do anything to me, Mother," insisted Noelle. "I punched him on the nose, remember?"

Her mother patted her cheek. "That's my girl," she said.

"I'm sorry your birthday weekend was ruined," said Noelle as she took her mother's arm and they proceeded down the hallway.

"Don't you worry about that," snapped Samantha. "My birthday is the least important thing right now. Why don't you come downstairs? Wallace wants to say goodbye to you before he leaves."

"Wallace?" she felt a bit angry, even saying his name, but she hadn't told her mother what her friend had done to offend her and she wasn't planning on revealing that information to anyone.

She braced herself and headed down the stairs into the parlor. Her mother excused herself, saying she needed a drink of water and left her alone. Noelle was very grateful.

Wallace spun around as soon as she entered the room. He looked so pale beneath his freckles that his skin was almost translucent.

"Noelle!" he rushed forward, but she held up a hand, her anger only just remaining in check. She could tell that he could see her fury in her eyes. He took a step back and folded his hands formally behind his back, his expression one of complete and utter repentance.

"You are rather despicable, you know," said Noelle, frowning at him. "How could you do that to me? Allow an acquaintance of mine to think I was some sort of common doxy. You're supposed to be my friend."

"I am, 'Elle!" cried Wallace, his cheeks reddening. "I just—."

"He was jealous."

Noelle spun around. Kenneth Black was standing in the parlor room doorway, his crooked grin firmly in place and his eyes sharp. "I suppose it was my fault," said Kenneth. He sidled up to them and sat himself down on the sofa. "I'm sorry, Gerson. I never should have driven you to such acts."

Wallace was staring at Kenneth.

Noelle giggled and Wallace raised his eyebrows at her.

"Oh, Kenneth, do be fair," she said.

Kenneth smiled ostentatiously. "Very well," he said, bowing his head. "Wallace Gerson, my name is Kenneth Black. I own a bakery on 6th Avenue in town. Feel free to stop by for a visit. I'm told it's a personal favorite of Miss Noelle's. You might just see her there from time to time."

"You..." Wallace seemed to be a little lost for words. "You're not an architect then?"

"No, he isn't," said Noelle. "We made that story up together."

"Ah," said Wallace, swallowing. "Right. He focused his attention on Kenneth. "Mr. Black, could I please have a moment with Miss Noelle?"

Kenneth gestured his hand forward as if to say: "By all means."

Wallace waited for Kenneth to leave the room, but the man was incorrigible.

"Alone," said Wallace pointedly. He was quickly becoming frustrated.

"I'm confused."

Noelle had to laugh, she couldn't help herself. "Come, Wallace, let's just step out into the hall."

With a sigh and a glare in Kenneth's direction, Wallace moved out into the foyer. As Noelle shut the door behind him, he opened his mouth. She knew that he was about to apologize, and suddenly found that she didn't need to hear it.

She held up her hand. "Wallace, you have always been a good friend to me," she said softly. "I'm sorry, but I don't think we will ever be more than friends."

Wallace's eyes went wide. "It is because I..."

"No, Wallace, dear."

Her friend nodded, and then smiled. "For what it's worth, I know my behavior has been despicable, and I am sorry."

"I know you are," said Noelle. She pressed a small kiss to his cheek.

At that moment, several guests tramped down the stairs. Noelle tugged on the long sleeves of the blouse she was wearing to be sure that the rope marks on her wrists were well hidden.

Amelia Gene Stovich was looking highly distressed as she came galumphing into the foyer.

"My dear!" she exclaimed on catching sight of Noelle. "My dear! How is your father? How are you?! What a dreadful catastrophe."

"Amelia," said Noelle, warmly. "We're all fine, thank you. I'm so sorry that the party had to be cut short."

Amelia waved a dismissive hand. "I wouldn't have expected anything less," she said. "I did want to ask you though, was there any word amongst your servants about my necklace?"

"Oh," Noelle had nearly forgotten the matter. "Oh, Amelia, I'm so sorry. I know how precious it was to you and Reginald, but I haven't heard a peep." I'll run and ask before you leave, shall I?

"Please, yes!"

"You've lost something, Mrs. Stovich?" Wallace had moved forward. Noelle remembered his missing coat buttons and nearly groaned.

The Forth family was moving down the stairs now, carrying their own luggage. "Cornella, Kimberly," Noelle greeted them looking around. "Have you misplaced your footmen? Let me get someone to help you with your cases."

Noelle stretched out a hand to take Mrs. Forth's suitcase from her, but the woman snatched it back out of her reach.

"Oh, no thank you, Miss Noelle," she said with a tight-lipped smile. "We're quite alright— Oh!" Cornella Forth's foot slipped on the bottom step and her case tumbled out of her fingers. It burst as it hit the ground and a cacophony of clatters and bangs echoed around the hall.

Kenneth came flying out of the parlor. Noelle noticed that he looked absolutely terrified. "What's going—," he broke off as Cornella Forth burst into tears.

Lying at the bottom of the staircase, scattered around the Forth family's feet, were piles of gold and silver baubles. Noelle watched as a golden button rolled across the floor and come to a halt beside Wallace. He stooped to pick it up.

"My necklace!" cried Amelia Gene Stovich, sounding outraged. She bent to retrieve a black velvet jewelry box from the clutter.

"Oh, Miss Cornella, how could you?" asked Noelle. She didn't know what to say.

"I-I'm so sorry, everyone," Mrs. Forth sobbed. "W-we didn't have any choice!"

Mr. Forth stepped forward. "Please forgive us," he said. "We're about to lose our home to the bank. Things are not going well for us, not at all." He shook his head. "I'm sorry." He stooped, packed his wife's clothes into her bag, leaving behind everything they had taken, and with a hand at her back, guided her out the front door.

"Wait!" It was Amelia. She had stepped forward.

"You poor dears," she said, and she embraced Cornella, who was still sobbing. "Look, my darling, look." And Noelle, in high astonishment, saw Amelia holding out her necklace. "Have it," she whispered. "Have it. And may better luck come your way in the future."

Cornella shook her head. "No, no, no," she said through her sobs. "Please. I couldn't."

"I insist!" boomed Amelia. There was nothing more to say about it. Cornella accepted the gift with a tremulous smile.

Noelle stepped toward Kimberly. "Here," she said quietly. She unclasped her own necklace and yanked off her ear bobs, knowing they were worth a small fortune. "For you," she said.

Wallace had gathered his gold buttons into his hands, and he passed them to Mr. Forth. "Here," he said, clasping the man's hand. "I hope it helps. Remember, you have friends here."

Mr. Forth was looking a bit teary-eyed himself. "Thank you," he said, his lower lip trembling. "Thank you all very much."

With that, he bundled himself, his wife and his daughter into their carriage, and set off down the drive.

"Well," said Kenneth, leaning against the parlor room door with a crooked smile on his handsome face. "That was interesting."

EPILOGUE

IN THE WEEKS TO come, Noelle would never understand quite how she had managed to pull herself together. She assumed it had everything to do with Kenneth's unyielding presence. It gave her something to look forward to each day, and his visits brightened even the darkest corners of her imagination. He seemed to carry the sun around in his pocket.

Kenneth packed his belongings and left the house to a roar of sound. Cynthia had been true to her word. He was thronged with journalists everywhere he went, asking him to tell the story of his heroic endeavor to save Noelle's life.

He was forced to close La Petite Paradis for several days, and Noelle's father, on learning this, hired a trio of professional guards to keep the "rumor-mongers" in check. After two days, Thomas invited Kenneth back to the house.

"There's no point in you staying there if you can't run your business," he said sourly. "Let everything calm down for a week or two."

When Kenneth protested, Thomas shouted him down, and Noelle was more than pleased.

"That was kind of you," Noelle said to her Father, "asking him to stay."

Thomas Brittler's eyes went very soft. "He saved my girl. My stubborn, ridiculous girl, who thought she could handle everything on her own," he sighed, shaking his head. "I owe the man my life. The least that I can do is offer him houseroom until this whole thing blows over."

Noelle smiled. Her mother and father had been so furious with her, so terrified for her. She felt horrible for causing them such grief. Charlotte and Sarah-Jane hadn't been any better. But they'd all saved their lectures, and she was very grateful they had. She'd also managed to convince them not to write and tell Dianna what had happened.

"What good would it do? She can't be here," she pleaded with them. "It will only make her frustrated and terrified. Don't tell her."

And in the end, they had agreed.

Her body ached in places she hadn't even realized that she had. The last few mornings, she had stayed abed well-past the acceptable hour and rose feeling a bit better each day.

Kenneth met her at the top of the stairs a week after the incident. "Alice said you were getting up," he mumbled, smiling sheepishly. "Might I join you for breakfast?"

"Yes, I think so," Noelle responded, covering a yawn. She took his arm, and they made slow progress down the stairs into the hall, Noelle wincing on every other step.

Her right ankle, the one Jeb had seized during her failed escape attempt, was a bit swollen and tender. By the time they reached the landing, Kenneth was looking at her with some concern.

"I suppose you would object if I carried you the rest of the way," he said, looking doubtful.

"Of course I wou—ahh!"

Kenneth had stooped without warning and gathered Noelle up into his arms. She was so shocked that she did little more than squeak in protest before he plodded down the remaining steps and set her gently on her feet in the foyer.

"Kenneth!" Noelle squawked, slapping at his shoulder. "I was more than capable—."

"Yes, I could see that," he interrupted, raising an eyebrow at her. "But I'm quite sure that it would have been dinner time before we would have made it down those last couple of steps."

Noelle looked back up the way they had come. "Rubbish," she said to him, and then she folded her arms and stalked towards the kitchen, her cheeks so pink she knew it must look as though she had rouged them.

Kenneth caught up to her after a moment and they entered the kitchen together. Marcia was in the middle of the room, wagging her finger at one of the kitchen maids, but on catching sight of Noelle's face, she stopped talking mid-sentence and bustled over to her.

"Oh, my dear. Oh, my, you're so pink. Are you fevered? Should we call for the doctor?"

Kenneth cleared his throat into his closed fist, masking his grin.

The next day Noelle found Kenneth standing at the head of the stairs once more. "Alice told me you were—."

"Getting up? Did you offer to pay her so that she would report my schedule to you?"

Kenneth laughed. "Breakfast?"

She nodded eagerly and turned towards the stairs, holding tight to the banister, but before she could do more than totter onto the first step, Kenneth had scooped her up into his arms once more.

"Hold on to me," he demanded, and Noelle, her cheeks just as red as they had been the day before, placed her arms around his neck.

He was smiling down at her, evidently quite pleased with himself, and then his grin slipped a little. Their faces were inches apart, and she could feel his breath tickling the tip of her nose.

"Maybe, you should put me down," she whispered.

"I don't think so," said Kenneth. "Noelle Brittler, you are utterly mad if you think I will ever let you go again." He tilted his head down and pressed a tentative kiss to her forehead, then, without looking at her, he began moving down the stairs.

"Well, this is quite interesting, isn't it?"

Noelle felt Kenneth's arm twitch beneath her.

"Tell me, Mr. Black," said Samantha Brittler, plodding slowly down the steps so that she could continue to look down on upon them. "Are you in the habit of sweeping any woman you meet off her feet?"

Noelle stared up at her mother. "I've been struggling on the steps," she explained.

"I see." Noelle's mother had a way of making you think you had done something wrong, even if you hadn't. She continued her descent, her eyes on Noelle's swollen ankle.

Noelle couldn't be sure, but she thought she saw the frown on her mother's face lessen slightly. Then she had moved past the place were Kenneth stood, frozen with Noelle in his arms. She was on the landing when she turned to look up at them, and Noelle heard Kenneth swallow roughly.

Samantha Brittler was eyeing her youngest daughter, and Noelle was waiting for the explosion. But then, suddenly, her mother smiled a sad, half-smile that didn't quite reach her eyes. "At least he's not an Indian," she said. And, chuckling to herself and shaking her head, she made her way downstairs and entered Thomas Brittler's office.

Noelle didn't know what to make of it. Neither, it appeared, did Kenneth. He stared after Samantha Brittler with his mouth hanging open.

With a small giggle at the look of incredulity on his face, Noelle said: "I think that may have been her way of telling you that she approves of you."

"An Indian?" asked Kenneth. He reached the bottom step, and let Noelle's feet touch down, keeping her close.

"Oh, of course, you wouldn't know," she said, looking up into his face. "My eldest sister, Dianna, has ran off with an Indian man somewhere in the Wyoming territory. It's really quite the scandal," her left hand lifted to hide her smug smile. "I suppose my interest in Manhattan's finest Baker pales by comparison."

"Your interest?" said Kenneth thoughtfully, brushing aside the fact that Noelle's elder sister was married to an American savage. "Well, I quite like the sound of that."

~

"It was understandable," Kenneth said. They were sitting on the lounge in the upstairs library a few days later, and Thomas, who had come for a visit, was playing with a toy train on the floor in front of them. "One moment we were in the garden..." he smiled at her, his eyes twinkling with mischief, "the next I was glaring at you from around every corner. I wouldn't have known what to think either!"

Noelle sighed and rubbed her wrist. She still bore the marks of the ropes she had fought to free herself from, but strangely, she didn't feel forced to hide them in front of Kenneth.

"How is she?" she asked after a moment. Her voice was quiet, and she knew Kenneth would understand about whom she was speaking.

His next breath was weighed down with grief. "Cynthia's calmed down quite a lot," he said. He shook his head, and Noelle saw the raw pain in his eyes. "I never knew," he said. "I'm her brother, I should have known she wasn't well."

"If she never told you, how could you know?"

"The doctors say she doesn't sleep. She's eating, but she's displaying signs of mental instability," he sighed and let his head fall back on the chair.

"I'm so sorry for what she did to you," he said. "I had no idea..."

Noelle couldn't bear to watch him fret. She placed her palm against his cheek. "It's alright. Everything's alright. Things will get better."

Kenneth leaned into her touch and opened his eyes. They were full of a steady heat. "If she'd hurt you, I never would have forgiven myself."

Noelle stood up and took Kenneth's hands in her own. "But see?" she said, pulling him off the couch so that he was standing amidst her flowing skirts. "I'm fine." She pressed a kiss to his knuckles.

"Thank the Lord," said Kenneth, and he bent his head to peer into her eyes. "I would have lost *my mind* if I had lost you. I nearly did, when I thought I had."

Noelle blushed. The barriers that had once stood between them, the issue of an impossible future, seemed to have vanished from her mind. Her father had raised no objections to Kenneth and Noelle spending time together, and her mother was holding her tongue. The dreams Noelle had always cherished, dreams of a future with a man who loved her… they all suddenly seemed so tangible. So… real.

"Noelle," he swallowed. "I understand, that I have very little to offer you. I'm not a wealthy man or one of particularly good standing… but I can't… I can't bear the thought of living without you. I had to face it, twice the last few days, and even when I was so angry with you I thought that I would go mad… Noelle, I *still* wanted you."

Noelle stared at him, her eyes wide.

"I'm not saying…" Kenneth drew a ragged breath and released one of her hands to scrub his fingers through his hair, and she saw a sudden flash of anger in his eyes. "I positively despise that man, Gerson," he growled finally.

Noelle laughed. She couldn't help it.

"I was so jealous!" he hissed, and his hands dropped to her waist, pulling her hips close to his with abandon. "I've never felt so murderous in all my life."

He looked down at her, and with fire still dancing in his eyes, he kissed her.

Suddenly, Noelle was on fire too. She was trembling in his arms as he held her, and his lips declared ownership of hers with a sense of triumph and victory. He was all she could feel. Kenneth, the heat of him. Her hands lying flat against his chest. She could feel his heartbeat. And she wanted to stand there and be kissed by him forever, because nothing else mattered but the taste of his lips roving over hers.

"Auntie Nell?" Thomas had abandoned his train and was tugging on her hem. "Auntie Nell."

"Hmm?" Noelle pulled away from Kenneth and looked down at her sister's son in utter confusion. He gestured for her to lean down so that he could whisper in her ear. "Cookie?"

Noelle laughed and looked up at Kenneth. "Thomas has requested a cookie, and I'm not about to tell him no," she said to him, smiling from ear to ear.

"Well, we can't keep the master waiting!" Kenneth bent and hefted Thomas into his arms. Noelle stood back and watched them gallop around the room, Kenneth pausing to wink at her as he went. Thomas's squeal of delight echoed off the tall library shelves.

Noelle stood stunned long after they had passed out of sight, staring at the door. Her heart had leapt into her throat at the sight of her nephew — who looked rather a lot like his grandfather— in the arms of the man she loved.

Loved.

The moment her mind had formed around the word she knew it was true. She was desperately, irrevocably in love with Kenneth Black. She wanted him more than she had ever wanted anything in her entire life. She cared nothing for what the world would think of her. She wanted him beside her, forever and always, and she said a prayer of thanks right then and there as tears began rolling down her cheeks.

"Auntie Nell!!" sang Thomas from down the hall.

And Noelle, wiping at her streaming eyes, followed them out of the room.

The End

There's more to come! Stay up to date by signing up for Josephine Blake's Newsletter *and* recieve a FREE copy of *The Heart of Hope-A Brittler Sisters Prequel.*

AFTERWORD

Dear reader,

I hope very much that you enjoyed every moment of Noelle's story. Noelle is a spirited, adventurous girl, and she's more like her sisters than I ever thought she would be. I had so much fun with her, and I hope you did too.

If you happen to have a moment, I would really appreciate it if you took a second to leave a review for *Noelle.* I read every review my books ever receive, and your feedback not only helps me to reach out to fantastic readers like you, but also to grow as a writer.

The Brittler Sisters was the first of many fun and exciting series that I hope to bring to you. Keep a look out for my *next release* due out in October 2017!

XOXO

About the Author

Josephine Blake is a *USA Today* Bestselling Author and an Award-Winning Graphic Designer. She enjoys a quiet life on a comfortable piece of property in her very own small-town in the Willamette Valley.

With over 20 published books in the romance genre, Josephine works hard to make sure her stories bring a little more love into this crazy world.

She and her husband spend most days chasing their little one around their farmhouse with thankful hearts.

Notable Works:

Josephine Blake's debut Historical Romance novel, *Dianna*, hit the shelves in August of 2016 and became a bestseller two years later. Her Gothic Historical Romance novel, *A Brush with Death*, followed suit later that year in 2018. Yours at Yuletide became her very first Contemporary Romance release in the winter of 2019.

Sign Up for her newsletter to stay up to date on every new release at www.awordfromjosephineblake.com.

Also by Josephine Blake

The Brittler Sisters Series

Dianna

Little Rose

Charlotte

Sarah-Jane

Noelle

The Heart of Hope

The Brides of Adoration

Maid in the West

Cowboy, Take Me Away

The Arms of a Stranger

Nursing His Heart

Sweet Love of Mine

Brenden's Bookish Bride

Love in Unity Springs

Yours at Yuletide

Second-Chance Santa

Mistletoe Miracles

Candy-Cane Kisses

Christmas in Unity Springs-Series Collection

Standalones

Two Hearts, One Stone

Multi-Author Projects

The ABC Mail Order Brides-Emeline's Exile

Charming Tales-Little Red
Silverpines Series-Wanted: Lawyer and Wanted: St. Nick

Josephine Blake also Writes Gothic Victorian Romance under her middle name, Elizabeth.

Titles by Elizabeth Blake

The Hands of Fate Series

A Brush with Death

A Twist of Fortune

A String of Lies

Standalones

Dark was the Night

www.ingramcontent.com/pod-product-compliance
Lightning Source LLC
Chambersburg PA
CBHW012017110726
47994CB00009B/3199

* 9 7 9 8 3 3 0 2 9 9 8 8 1 *